TRI-TIP

GRADE-A BEEFCAKES SERIES - BOOK 3

VANESSA VALE

Tri-Tip

Copyright © 2018 by Vanessa Vale

Cover design: Bridger Media

Cover graphic: Deposit Photos: ysbrand; Period Images

GET A FREE BOOK!

JOIN MY MAILING LIST TO BE THE FIRST TO KNOW OF NEW RELEASES, FREE BOOKS, SPECIAL PRICES AND OTHER AUTHOR GIVEAWAYS.

http://freeromanceread.com

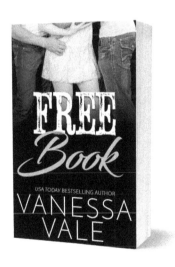

PROLOGUE

I was happy for Duke and T. Fucking happy they'd found their women. Duke and Jed doted on Kaitlyn like she was a piece of fragile china. Tucker and Colton were given a run for their money with Ava. Instant, insane love. Just like our dad had told us would happen. That didn't mean I wasn't jealous. If those fuckers could get a woman to not only *like* them, but fall in love with them, then they knew better than to let her go. Except I wasn't going to claim a woman with just one best friend. No, I had the twisted need to share her with two. I'd assumed the *her* would never appear. What chick would want to deal with *three* guys? If she were out there, I'd never seen her before.

Or so I'd thought...

PARKER

"*E*asy, boy. I won't hurt you," I murmured, trying my gentlest voice.

I stared down some kind of brown mutt who looked like he was about to bolt. There was nowhere for him to go out on the prairie like this. Just open fields and then beyond those, even more empty expanses. He seemed like a nice dog and was probably hungry.

Glancing about, I wondered where he could get water. A creek? There were cottonwood trees in the distance which meant water, but still. Some loser must've dumped him on the side of the road.

His brown eyes met mine, his body still, muscles tense and quivering.

"You want a sandwich? I'll share."

I backed up slowly so he wouldn't run off—I couldn't leave him out here, and I didn't want to chase after him—and pulled out my wrapped ham sandwich from the center console.

Taking out half, I tossed it toward him. He jumped back, then sniffed.

I went to the back door of the cruiser and opened it up, tossing the other half on the plastic seat. He wasn't a prisoner, but he needed a bath before he sat up front.

I leaned against the side of the SUV and looked away so I didn't spook him.

Out of the corner of my eye, I saw him debating before tiptoeing—if dogs did that—toward the sandwich on the ground and gobbling it down. Lifting his head, he sniffed the air. He was no dummy and knew exactly where the other half was. I just had to hope he was smart enough to climb in to get it.

He was. He hopped into the back to get the rest of his snack. I shut the door and went around to the driver's seat, settled behind the wheel.

"Pam, I'm out on County Road Seven and picked up a stray dog. Hungry. I think he should be seen by a vet," I said into my police radio.

"There's a place on Fourth, two blocks off of Main," she replied, her voice tinny through the speaker.

I glanced into the back where the dog was licking his lips, clearly having enjoyed the sandwich more than I would have. He sat his butt down on the seat and stared at me, cocked his head to the side. Part lab, part basset hound, part... what did I know about dogs other than this one was tan? I'd never had one growing up. He seemed content in his spot, as if he'd ridden in a car often enough and knew he was going somewhere. And that he wasn't alone.

Yeah, I could relate, buddy.

It felt good to be wanted, to have someone take care of you—and by that I meant pressing me up against the door or bending me over the bed when I came home from work and making me forget about every single call or court appearance. I wanted him to help me out of my bland uniform and get me naked. To take control so I could submit. Let go. Give over.

God, yes.

And by *him* I meant two guys because one wasn't enough for me. I needed the extra helping of dominance, the constant potency my high-revving libido needed.

I wasn't neglected—my vibrator saw to that—or abandoned on the side of the road like the furry guy eyeing me. I was back in my hometown, had a new job, my mom was nearby and I had plenty of batteries for the well-used sex toy... there was nothing to complain about. But while I wasn't alone, I— make that my pussy—was definitely a little lonely.

Dick would be nice. Double dick, preferably, because I had a lot to offer. I had a feeling I was too much for just one guy because I had *a lot* to offer. Momma called me big-boned. I considered myself more Amazon than anything. At just under six feet, I towered over most guys in town. And those big bones? Yeah, on top of them I had muscles and a fair amount of padding. Big boobs, big butt. Not too many men were interested in all that I came with. I'd had boyfriends—I was far from a virgin—but it had been a while. I was discriminate and was definitely picky when it came to who got in my bed. Or pressed me up against the wall.

Then there was the fact that I was the sheriff of Raines County and that came with a utility belt, a set of handcuffs and a uniform shirt that had me looking more man than woman. I wasn't the soft, timid type. I wasn't dainty. Petite. Most men wanted to wear the pants in a relationship and my job didn't call for skirts. Jeans, boots and the uniform shirt. Even a utility belt with more gadgets than Batman.

I sighed. The job picked me and here I was. Raines, Montana, in a sheriff's SUV with a stray dog. I doubted I'd find one man, let alone two, at least while I had the job. I made a mental note to add more batteries to my shopping list. I was going to need them.

"Ten-four," I replied, putting the radio away and starting back toward town. Every day on the job was different. Paperwork, time in court, traffic stops. Hell, even a dog rescue. For being a small town, the job wasn't boring. So far, not too bad. Back in law school, I never would have imagined myself back in my hometown. Gone ten years, back two months.

I glanced in the rearview mirror and eyed the dog. I wanted to go and track down the fucker who'd abandoned him, but parked in front of the small vet office instead. "I'm going inside for a leash," I told him as I glanced at him through the metal grate between the front and back. One ear pointed up as if he were listening carefully. "No way am I chasing you all over town."

I climbed out, went inside. A little bell above the door signaled my presence. There was no one at the counter, but a guy came down a long hallway.

Not just any guy. Holy shit.

Gus Duke.

We'd dated—if eighteen-year-olds called it dating—right after high school graduation and most of that summer. First love. First everything. We'd been hot and heavy most of the time, especially when he'd popped my cherry in his pickup truck down a dusty side road late one night. I'd popped his, too. It had been intense—the feelings, the desire we shared that one hot summer. God, I'd *needed* what Gus would give me, loved every minute of it, of that steamy summer.

But as I grew older, I realized what we'd done wasn't enough for me. I was different, had unusual sexual desires. It was almost as if I were wired differently. Vanilla wasn't for me.

Thinking back, I had to wonder if we'd had more time together we might have done more than fuck like rabbits. Hot, hard and heavy. Come August, we'd both gone off to college and never looked back. Oh, I'd thought about him often enough. The sex, especially. We'd been horny teenagers interested in getting off and not the nuances of how to do that. It had taken years for me to understand it was better when it pushed all the right hot buttons. I had to wonder if Gus would know how to push mine... or if he'd want to. Especially when I realized, even staring at his gorgeousness now, he wouldn't be enough.

At eighteen, he'd been cute. Hot. Sexy, even. But now, he looked amazing. He'd always been tall—that was one of the things I'd liked about him, making me feel almost short—but at twenty-eight, he'd filled out, added about thirty pounds of lean muscle that couldn't be missed in his snug jeans and the cut of his shirt.

I'd seen him once since I'd been back. There had been an incident at the Duke ranch, a trespasser, and they'd called it in. Gus's brother, Tucker, now ran things, but the whole family had been there for a picnic. I'd been on shift and shown up with a deputy who'd been ready to take the guy down if necessary. It hadn't been since the asshole—I could confirm he was one based on the filth he'd spewed the entire time he was in custody—had been trussed up like a Christmas goose when we arrived. So I'd done nothing more than give Gus a small wave of greeting—and he'd offered me a wink in return—before we took the guy away. I hadn't had a chance to look my fill.

But now I could. And did.

Dark hair, dark eyes that were eyeing me as closely as I was him. The beard was new—I doubted he'd had more than a few whiskers at eighteen. Close-cropped, even from across the lobby I could see hints of red in it. He wore a flannel button-up and jeans. Sturdy leather boots. All he was missing to complete his full cowboy look was a hat, but I knew he had one since he'd had it on when I saw him at the Duke ranch. He didn't look like a veterinarian, but a calendar model for Sexy Cowboys of Montana.

"Parker," he said and nothing else. His deep voice crept into me and made my nipples hard. God, one word and I was in trouble here.

Ten years just fell away and I was that girl who had it bad… really bad for the sexy Duke boy. There was a decade worth of things to say, but I had no idea how to start.

Want to pick up where we left off? If I remembered correctly, I was naked and in the back of your pickup and you'd been happily between my parted thighs. Maybe a bed this time? And bring a friend!

That was my pussy thinking and she wasn't in charge. At least not right now, so I thumbed over my shoulder. "Gus. I... um, found a stray dog. Got him in my car. Thought maybe you could take a look at him."

He went over to a hook on the wall with a few rope leashes and took one down. "Sure. Let's go get him."

He escorted me out of the clinic, leaving the door open behind him. The weather was dry and warm, considering we were sliding into fall. I went to the SUV and he followed. When I opened the back door, I spied him eyeing my ass. He grinned, not the least bit ashamed at being caught. Yeah, he hadn't changed all that much.

Before Gus could get the leash on him, the dog jumped out, trotted up the walk to a small shrub, peed beside it, then continued right inside the vet office.

Gus watched and gave a little head shake. "Guess she's not going to be a difficult patient."

"She?" I asked, staring into the vet clinic as if I could still see the dog. "I thought *she* was a *he.*"

He glanced at me, the smile still on his full lips—the lips I remembered kissing me oh so well—and arched one dark brow. "*She* squatted to pee. Didn't lift a leg."

That made sense. "I didn't take time to check out her... undercarriage."

The dark brow went up higher and his full lip curled in that sexy way I remembered so fondly. "I remember *your* undercarriage." He took a step closer and I could smell him. Soap and outdoors and that familiar scent that was pure Gus. "Tell me, pixie, still got that little mole on the inside of your right thigh? Right up by those pretty pussy lips?"

2

GUS

*P*arker reached out and put a hand over my mouth and I smiled against her palm. Her cheeks flushed a bright red and the way her dark eyes flared not just with fire, but with heat, I had no doubt her pussy was soaking wet. Yeah, the first few words I said to her after a decade were about the little birthmark I'd seen up close and very, *very* personal. That summer

I'd spent a lot of time with my head between her parted thighs. I'd been the first to get them open, and I never forgot that sweet spot, kissing the little mark, then her juicy slit a little to the right.

It had been easy between us. Sure, we'd messed around and made fools of ourselves. Getting naked with someone the first time had been more fumbling than fucking. I doubted I'd lasted a minute after getting inside of Parker. But, she'd opened for me again, and again until I lasted a whole hell of a lot longer, and I'd made her scream my name.

I smiled now, even thinking about how passionate she was. Like a little firecracker, going off with the slightest bit of heat. I'd lit that fire, made her so fucking hot I'd pretty much been ruined for anyone else. But, the summer had been short and life got in the way.

College for both of us. Vet school for me. Law school for Parker. We were driven people, pushing for what we wanted, working hard and getting it. But she was the one who got away. No fucking doubt about it.

But she was back now. One glimpse of her at the ranch the week before had had me itching to see her again, to pick up where we left off all those years ago. Me, balls deep, and this time without any fumbling at all. And she'd meet me halfway, no question about it. I wouldn't have to coax her legs open. She'd fall back on my bed and spread them wide, eager for a wild ride.

Parker wasn't a meek little thing. Hell, no. I had to look down to have our eyes meet, but not by much. I wanted a woman who could hold her own, but wanted to submit, to give over her control. Parker was smart as fuck, had a career. Could stand on her own two feet without a man. But that didn't mean I didn't want to be the one in her life. Or, one of the ones.

Looking back, it was obvious she'd been into every kinky thing we'd tried after high school. But we'd been eighteen. Virgins. We'd known practically nothing, including what kind of sex we liked—other than straight fucking.

Now I liked it hard. Wild. And often. I wanted it with Parker. And hopefully, she'd like it the same way. *And* with Kemp and Poe. I just had to find out how interested she was in being with three men. Seeing interest—at least in me—plainly on her face was one thing. Having her say the words was another. And crucial.

I loved the feel of her hand on my mouth. Soft, warm. I could smell her clean scent. No perfume for Parker. Just fresh air, sunshine and something perfectly *her.* I started talking and she pulled her hand away. "You remember *my* undercarriage, I'm sure. It's pretty unforgettable." I patted my chest and grinned. "I grew some since I was eighteen. *Everywhere.*"

"Oh my god," she said, shaking her head and rolling her eyes.

I couldn't help but smile because there was the playful Parker I remembered. God, I'd missed her. My dick swelled just having her near. I wanted to get her out of that uniform and naked. Those handcuffs on her waist might come in handy for the things we could do together.

I didn't need to go for subtle. No candlelight dinner and sweet seduction. Parker didn't need it, or, if I knew her as well as I thought I did, want it.

"Remember that time I bent you over the back tailgate of my truck? It was the perfect height for me to fuck you. If I remember correctly, I slid my thumb in your ass."

Her mouth fell open and I could tell she remembered. Good.

"Are you like this with all your clients?"

"Since you got back to town, pixie?" I asked, looking her over. I was blatant about it, too. I wanted her to know I liked what I saw, that I'd noticed the way she'd filled out even more since eighteen. If she did a thorough pass of me, she'd see just how hard I was for her. "Only you."

She flushed even more at that, like the young schoolgirl I remembered. She was tall and had curves that went on for miles. She was lush, more than a handful of tits and ass, thick thighs and fuck, I ached to be between them again.

Her straight hair was pulled back into a ponytail at the nape of her neck. Simple and plain, but it only showed off how beautiful she was. High cheekbones, fair skin that blushed so prettily and full lips I remembered wrapping around my dick.

Her eyes lowered and I said nothing, giving her the opportunity to look me over. I wasn't small, anywhere. As I'd said, I'd grown *everywhere* since I was eighteen. I'd been big back then… baby arm big if I remembered her words the first time she'd laid eyes on my dick, but now… I had to tuck it down along the inside of my thigh in order to walk comfortably. And at this moment, it was turning into a lead pipe. When her eyes widened, I grinned. Yeah, she'd seen it.

I put my hand on it, pressed down, hoping to hold off any pre-cum from spurting out. It would all be for Parker and I wasn't ashamed, but I wanted her to see I had a little more control than I'd had as a teenager.

Although with her, perhaps not so

much until I'd had her a few times. Her eyes settled on my left hand.

That's right, pixie. No wedding ring. I wouldn't flirt with her—or any woman —if I were taken. Hell, I *was* taken. By Parker. She just didn't know it yet.

She licked her lips. "I remember you. How it was. How could I forget? But that was a long time ago. I'm sure you've improved your technique a bit. I know I have mine."

Improved? Probably. Refined, definitely. The idea that she's been with other guys made me want to track each one of them down and rip their heads off. But I'd had other women, and I never expected her to sit at home and pine for me, her pussy all neglected. But once I got back inside her, those other guys would all be forgotten, that was for fucking sure.

But if she got any better at sex, she'd probably kill me. Her pussy had been magic before. But now... "Oh, pixie, it's been too long." My voice went all soft and quiet as I used the old nickname I had for her—she was the farthest thing from a pixie. Our conversation changed from playful banter to something... intimate. Something from so long ago, and yet it was as if a whole decade hadn't passed.

"There's a dog sitting on a chair in the waiting area."

"Holy shit, who's that?" Parker leaned in and whispered.

I'd seen Kemp before, so I watched Parker, took in her first impression of him. Yeah, I couldn't miss the interest there. Women practically tossed their panties at Kemp, with his calm demeanor and good looks. He was single, didn't live with his mother and as a vet, had a solid job. A total catch, but no one had snagged him yet. I was just hoping Parker would.

I glanced his way, saw him scratching his head, clearly amused by the dog. He was as tall as me, but a little leaner. Where I was dark, he was fair with blond, curly hair. He wore his usual black t-shirt and jeans. None of us went for the short, white vet coat.

"The sheriff dropped off our latest patient," I told him, but I looked back at Parker as I made introductions. "Kemp, meet Parker Drew."

"*The* Parker Drew?" he countered, then came down the walk.

"That's me," she replied, extending her hand to shake. "Temporary sheriff."

Hell yeah, I'd talked about Parker to Kemp and Poe. She was The One. I'd thought it after seeing her again at the ranch, and I was positive now. Just seeing her... all ball busting and sweetness rolled into one gorgeous package, and I knew Kemp had to agree.

I had a history with her, so I could talk dirty to her without being slapped. No, Parker wasn't one to slap. She'd knee me in the balls and then make earrings out of them. From the interest in her eyes, I was safe from that. I could talk about her pussy, let her know my dick was hard for her. It wasn't going to scare her off. It hadn't yet. If Kemp did so, he'd come across as a total sleaze. But I couldn't miss his interest.

"Either you're into county politics and I'm infamous in my new job or this guy's been blabbing," she said, pointing at me.

"I know since Sheriff Hogan died, the city council voted to hire a temporary replacement. Since it's an elected position, they decided to have someone fill the spot until November when people can decide who gets the job, either Hogan's son, Liam, or Mark

Beirstad. Or you. You're that replacement."

"That's right," she confirmed.

"But Gus did blab," he added with a wink. "It's nice to meet the ex-girlfriend. The one who got away."

Parker's mouth fell open and she stared at me with those big, dark eyes. I could read her mind: *The one who got away?* I shrugged, but didn't say anything. She hadn't dumped me. I hadn't broken up with her. We'd just run out of time. She'd headed to Vermont and I'd gone to Minnesota for college, both of us focused and driven when it came to school, and we'd grown apart. Moved on. Until now. Now we were going back and picking up where we left off. But this time, hopefully, with Kemp and Poe joining in on the fun.

"Tell me what's up with your dog." Kemp angled his head toward the building. It was clear Parker was glad he'd changed the topic. I'd come on strong and Kemp, while not being forward at all, was a lot for a woman to take in. The way Parker couldn't help but look him over proved that.

"Oh, he's... I mean, *she's* not mine. I found her out on County Road Seven. I brought her in to make sure she's all right."

He glanced behind him into the waiting area. "I'd like to drop the fucker who dumped her out there and see how he does without any food, water or shelter." He ran his hand over the back of his neck. "She doesn't look too rough, considering, so I'm guessing she hasn't been out there too long." He glanced at Parker, then me. "I'll take her in the back and see if she's chipped."

Kemp went back inside and we were alone.

"Any trouble with that trespasser?" she asked as if trying to make small talk.

I was amused. I could tell she was a little flustered, but hid it well. She was a past lover. More than that. Parker hadn't been a one-night stand. Far from it. We'd shared first love. Lots of firsts. It was a little awkward remembering what we'd done together, trying different positions in my old pickup truck, and a smile tugged at my lips at how fun it had been with her. Playing, discovering. Knowing she hadn't seen me at my finest.

She knew what I looked like naked, knew what I looked like when I came. We hadn't been all that adventurous since there weren't very many places we could have fooled around. I had three siblings and my house had always been crazy. There was no way we could have done anything in my room. And Parker's house? I'd snuck in once through her bedroom window, but we'd had to be really quiet since the place was small and the walls thin. And I'd learned that Parker was a screamer when she came, and that would have been bad with her mom down the hall. I knew she'd been close with her mom, but not *that* close.

I ran my fingers idly through my beard, and she watched as if she wished she could do it herself. "You know more about the charges than we do, but the guy hasn't been back." Some fucker had framed Ava's dad for insider trading and wanted to marry her to get the rest of her family's money. Which was a shit-ton. Ava had no interest in the guy, not even before she'd gotten hot and heavy with my brother, Tucker, and Colton Ridge. The guy had shown up at the ranch just to fuck with her, and that had pissed everyone off. "Ava doesn't have to worry about the loser anymore."

Besides Ava having the law on her side, she had the entire Duke family and other men like Colton, Jed and the ranch hands to keep an eye out. She might take Jed's name when they married, but she'd still belong to Tucker as well. She'd still be my sister-in-law. I wasn't sure how well Parker knew Ava, but maybe they'd met before, especially since Ava owned and ran the Seed and Feed.

"Things were a little crazy that day, but I wanted to talk with you," I added. Fuck, had I ever. And not just talked. One look at her after all these years and I'd wanted to toss her over my shoulder and carry her someplace private so we could get to know each other again... in all ways. Like whether she whimpered and still clenched right before she came. Or if she liked having her shoulder nipped as I took her from behind, like a stallion would a mare.

Get her on her knees and have her swallow me down as those dark eyes looked up at me.

But she'd been working and I had no intention of interfering with her job. After she left, I'd had to go and jerk off in the bathroom just like I had as a teenager.

She'd brought the dog to the clinic in her role as sheriff, so talking dirty might not be the best idea while she was working, but I didn't think the animal was going to tell anyone.

We walked inside and she took in the place. The three of us—me, Kemp and Poe—had met at vet school and decided early on we'd go into practice together and opened shop two years ago. Bought the building and the practice off of a woman who'd wanted to retire. Not only did we work together, we'd claim a woman together too, but up until Parker had returned to

Raines, we hadn't known who that would be.

Now we did. I wasn't sure how she'd go for it the idea of three guys claiming her. My oldest brother, Landon—nicknamed Duke even though it was all our last names—and Jed Cassidy, were in a relationship with the town librarian and should have made a stir. It wasn't like they gave a shit what people thought, but Kaitlyn wouldn't want to lose her job because of uptight townspeople. But right after they'd been pussy whipped, Tucker and Colton Ridge fell for Ava, even asked her to marry them. No one in town really seemed to care. My parents didn't. Hell, they were thrilled that grandchildren were possibilities.

I wasn't thinking kids with Parker... I had to get inside her again first, but based on how the town reacted to my brothers' relationships, she could still be sheriff—hopefully—and be with three men without anyone freaking out. But, her job depended on votes—if her name was on the ballot—so we had to think of image. But right now, staring at her, what I wanted with Parker was none of the town's damned business and no one was going to stop me.

"A little," she agreed with a smile.

I stared at her blankly for a moment, having forgotten what we'd been talking about. Right, her picking up Perry the Prick from the ranch.

"Have dinner with me," I said, done waiting. Having her in front of me made me want to grab her and never let go. But dinner was good. Smart. Talk first, fuck after. That was my brain thinking. My dick thought backwards was better. Fuck now, eat later.

She stopped in her tracks, turned and looked up at me, her mouth open as

if she were going to say—hopefully
—yes.

"No chip," Kemp called, walking out
of one of the exam rooms, not realizing
he'd pretty much cock blocked me.
Himself, too, in fact. The dog was right
at his side, tongue hanging out as if she
were smiling. "I did a test and no
worms either. Until someone left her
out in the middle of nowhere, she
appears to be well taken care of. Good
temperament. She's a little dehydrated
and probably could use a good meal—"

"She had my sandwich in the SUV,"
Parker said.

Kemp smiled. Oh, that smile had
dropped lots of panties in the past. I had
to hope it was at least making Parker's
wet.

"You must be hungry then. Come eat
with us," I offered. "The vet tech is on
her break and we're in the back room."

She glanced down at the radio on

her hip. Seeing as it was quiet, it wasn't as if she had to head out. "I could eat. Thanks."

This wasn't the dinner date I wanted, but it was immediate, and that was almost better since I wasn't ready for her to leave yet. And, she got to meet Kemp and Poe.

Kemp led us down the hallway and I watched as Parker took the opportunity to ogle Kemp's ass. I should have been pissed she was checking out another guy, but I was fine with it. At least fine that it was Kemp. I hoped that Parker was as kinky as me, and seeing her interest in me *and* Kemp gave me hope.

The dog trotted along beside Parker, happy as could be to hang with her. Smart girl.

"We have a guest for lunch," Kemp said as he walked into the kitchen. Parker stopped just inside the doorway when she saw Poe, clearly not expecting a third guy.

Poe stood and I watched as she tilted her head up to look him in the eye. He was the tallest of us at six-four.

I heard her whisper under her breath. "Oh shit." She turned to look at me, a little stunned and a whole lot flushed. "What's in the water around here?"

I chuckled, put my hand on her shoulder and nudged her into the kitchen. Our uneaten lunch—plastic containers of leftovers, a brown bag with sandwiches, chips and drinks— was spread out across the table.

Poe wiped his big hands on his jeans. "Hey there." His voice was deep, which could easily be used to intimidate, but the smile he gave Parker hopefully made him a little less formidable. But Parker didn't spook easily and she smiled back. "I'm Poe. The third vet around here."

"Like Edgar Allen?" she asked, cocking her head to the side.

Poe grinned. "My mother liked dark poetry."

"I'm Parker."

Poe looked to me, eyes wide, then looked her over with a new appreciation, a very blatant one. "*The* Parker?"

Parker glanced over her shoulder at me. "How much do you share with these two?"

"When it comes to you? I'll share *everything* with Kemp and Poe."

3

PARKER

*O*h. My. God.

I'll share everything with Kemp and Poe.

Did that mean... did they? Oh shit. All three of them were staring at me.

With the four of us together, the room felt small, like there was barely any oxygen. But it was the fact that they were too gorgeous for their own good that had me practically hyperventilating. My nipples hardened and I wondered what it would be like to have them strip me bare and... do whatever they wanted.

Not just one alpha male with Gus, but there was no question Kemp and Poe would be just as intense. Powerful. My pussy clenched at the thought.

Three hot men all eyeing me as if I were the lunch instead of what was on the table.

What exactly had Gus meant by those words?

Gus moved around me, pulled out a chair, but ignored my wide-eyed stare. "Sit."

I did and the guys pulled out their food and spread it out on the table so it was like a little buffet. Gus pointed. "There's leftover lasagna, a turkey sandwich with avocado, um... something green that Poe brought—"

"Kale salad." He tugged the container

away from Gus as if it weren't a bitter superfood but a sweet dessert.

"And leftover chocolate cake," Gus finished. "Although only store bought since my parents are on vacation."

Oh yes, there was a decadent slice of cake and my mouth watered.

"Gotta eat your veggies first," Poe grinned, waving about his container of salad. "Makes you grow big and strong."

His gaze raked over me in a heated way, recognizing I was already big and strong.

He had hair as black as night with a hint of curl. Blue eyes that were pale and piercing. Black Irish all the way, which completely and totally worked for me. Crazy, since Gus, with his beard and quick smile, was gorgeous. So was Kemp, all fair and seemingly gentle.

Oh shit, I was in big trouble lusting after three men. Three friends. Colleagues.

"The sandwich looks great," I answered, remaining neutral. "Thanks."

Kemp took one of the halves and placed it on a paper napkin and slid it across the linoleum surface to me.

"So tell us about yourself, how you ended up being sheriff," Poe asked.

I glanced at his pale eyes and saw he was interested and really wanted to know. He wasn't one of the guys who patronized me. *What's a gal like you doing with a big gun? Are you a lesbian or something?*

"You want me to recap the past ten years?" I asked.

He shrugged. "Tell us anything you want."

I swallowed. As sheriff, I was the one who asked the questions, did the interrogating. "Well, Gus headed to Minnesota for college, I went to Vermont. Dartmouth. From there, law school. I always wanted to be a lawyer."

"I remember," Gus replied. "And I always wanted to be a vet. That's why we went our separate ways. We were both driven. We had big plans, didn't we, pixie?"

We had. And now that I was sitting before Gus again, I realized how thankful I was for him. He had wanted me to go after what I wanted and hadn't held me back. We'd given up *us* for... well, us.

"Yes. Now look at us."

"Yeah, but explain the sheriff part," Poe continued.

It seemed that was what he was really interested in.

"I was an assistant district attorney back east. They wanted closer interaction with the police department... the new chief thought it would better if someone from the DA's office could work closely with the cops. Ensure their procedures were accurate so they didn't have cases fall apart because procedure wasn't followed."

"That makes sense," Gus commented.

I nodded. "It did. My boss was really happy with that. The police wanted a DA to understand them better. So they offered to send someone to the police academy. That was me. To make a long story short, I was looking to move back to Raines because of my mom—she's fine, but she's diabetic now, and I felt too far away if something went wrong —and I'm sure she talked to your mother or someone else on the city council and they called me about the position."

Gus grinned. "Yeah, I have no doubt the mom network certainly helped get your name on the short list. But your resume's what got you the job."

Not even the dimmest bulb would hire a sheriff who wasn't qualified.

"I'm more lawyer than lawman. That's why I don't go on calls alone. One of the deputies is always with me. I made that a requirement of employment."

Poe made a grunt, as if he either was satisfied with the answer or hated it and didn't want to say.

"What about you?" I asked him, taking a bit of the sandwich, eager to take the spotlight off of me. I'd rather hear about what made him brooding and... well, smoldering. Those pale eyes had me hooked.

"Me? Let's talk about Gus. I heard you were his first." Poe speared his salad as if he were commenting on the weather, not his co-worker's sexual initiation. With me.

The sandwich was halfway to my mouth for a second bite and I froze, glanced at Gus. "Jesus. You told them?"

He grabbed the lasagna container

and stuck it in the microwave, then leaned his hip against the counter. "Hell, yeah."

"Hell, yeah?" I replied.

"I was excited to hear you were back in town."

"So you told them we had sex," I clarified. "That's quite a leap."

The corner of his mouth tipped up. I remembered that small gesture, how it made me climb in his lap and kiss him. And then do more. He'd loved to lean in and suck on my nipples until I was writhing. Only then did he let me sink onto him and ride him like a cowgirl.

"I told them I wanted sex with you again."

The microwave dinged and he looked away to get the food. The scent of tomato sauce and garlic filled the air.

Heat pooled low in my belly at his words. He wanted me. There was no confusion on that. I put the sandwich down. "So you're looking for, what? One wild night?"

"Who said anything about just one night?" he asked, coming to sit at the table with his reheated food. Our knees bumped beneath the table.

I stared at Gus. Waited. Tried to calm my racing heart because I was all for sex with him again.

He glanced at me, grabbed a fork from the center of the table where there was a little utensil holder. "I loved you, pixie. I always have. No woman's ever come close to you, or what we shared. I guess I've just been waiting."

Holy. Shit. He loved me?

"You... you don't know anything about me," I countered. I felt ridiculously nervous and a little excited. It was a little weird to have this conversation in front of Kemp and Poe, but they seemed to be enjoying themselves as they watched, Poe eating his salad. Kemp just grinned.

"You just told us a bunch." Gus leaned in. "I know more about you than most people."

Would I ever stop blushing? Would I ever stop remembering what his lips had felt like on mine... and other places? Was his beard as soft as it looked? Would it tickle the inside of my thighs as he ate me out? God, I wanted him to skip the Italian and go right for my pussy instead.

"But I want to learn more," he continued. "That's why I asked you to dinner."

"And after?" I asked. He'd flirted. He'd talked about his... undercarriage. Hadn't hidden how aroused he was. Sex was open for discussion, even in front of Kemp and Poe.

His eyes dropped to my mouth. "After, I want to touch you again. Find all your sweet spots. Touch them, lick them. Make you come. Fuck, do I ever."

I swallowed hard, thrilled I hadn't eaten much of the sandwich yet. My skin heated, and I knew I was blushing.

"It was good between us," he continued. "But we barely had time to figure out what made us hot."

"You made me hot," I replied honestly, which made him smile, his gaze dropped to my mouth. If I'd said anything else, he'd know it was a lie. "But you're right, I've learned some stuff about what I like. I'm not sure—"

"If what, I'll be into it?" He forked up a piece of lasagna, stuck it in his mouth.

I glanced at Kemp and Poe, saw their quiet curiosity. Heated, and interested, gazes. It probably wasn't very often they had this kind of conversation over lunch at the office.

"Well, yeah."

He tipped his chin up, indicating I

should eat. I picked up the half
sandwich again, took another bite.
Chewed. I was thankful for the moment
to organize my thoughts.

What the hell was going on? In the
space of a few minutes, I'd run into Gus
again, ex-boyfriend and virginity
claimer. I'd met his two vet colleagues
who were smoking hot and seemed to
know more about me than I ever
imagined. And I was sitting here... in
front of two other men, talking about
what it would be like if Gus and I had
sex again. It would definitely be hot and
heavy, but I didn't know if it would be
enough. I had no doubt he'd make me
come every time. He had ten years ago.

Okay, not that first time because it
had hurt like hell, but that missed
orgasm had been his motivation to see
me satisfied every time after that. And
he'd gone after it with a boyish
enthusiasm that I'd found endearing.

Now, there was no doubt he'd pleasure me not only with that same eagerness, but with skill that only came with experience. A wicked combination.

Still… it wasn't going to be enough. I needed more. I craved it.

I was single. It had been awhile since I'd had an honest to goodness, male-induced orgasm. And Gus's dick? Oh yeah, I wanted some of that grown up piece of meat, but I didn't know if he could give me what I wanted. If he even was into the same things as me. Just because we'd been good together at eighteen didn't mean it would be the same—or better—now. I *was* wired for a little kink. No, a lot of kink. To top it off, I wasn't just attracted to Gus. I glanced at Kemp and Poe. I wanted them too.

"Okay, so share some stuff that you're into," he said calmly, as if he were asking me to talk about my favorite books. My preferred jelly flavor. If I liked mint or gel toothpaste.

I glanced between the three of them.

Kemp sat back in his chair as if he were settling in for a while. Poe completely ignored his green salad and watched me.

"How did me bringing a stray dog to the vet turn into a lunchtime chat about my sex life?"

I glanced down, saw the dog in question curled up and sleeping at my feet. A matchmaking dog? Her job was done and now she rested.

"Because, sweetheart, Gus shares a lot of things," Poe said, setting his forearms on the table and leaning in. Getting *really* close. "If Gus can't do it for you, I can." He patted his broad chest and grinned. What a ruthless smile. He could use it like a weapon.

Women toss their panties at him for that look aimed at them.

"Me, too," Kemp added. "You've seen Gus's dick. It's the smallest in the room."

"You guys are assholes," Gus muttered, taking the ribbing good-naturedly. He had nothing to be ashamed about, that was for sure. I remembered him being big enough where I couldn't have closed my grip around his thick girth. But if the other guys were bigger...

"Are you telling us he wasn't that great?" Poe wondered. "I mean, first couple of times and all."

Gus held up his hands. "Hey, now. I was the perfect gentleman. The lady comes first." He'd certainly seen to that.

"You're not saying anything." Kemp was eyeing me, waiting. "It wasn't great?" he prompted, then laughed. "Maybe Poe and I need to give Gus a few pointers. We get you between us and he can watch. Learn."

I sucked in a breath at what he was suggesting.

Gus eyed me very closely, as if my answer impacted his entire sexual identity. After all this time, he seemed confident he'd done me right, but now... his friends were obviously making him doubt.

"Baby girl, remaining quiet is like waving a red cape at a bull," Kemp added.

I tried not to smile at the way Gus looked, half horrified that he might have left me unsatisfied, and half pissed that his friends were intentionally riling him.

"You were great," I finally said, patting his hand and picking up my sandwich, not addressing Kemp's comment.

Gus gave a little grunt as way of

responding, then shoveled in a forkful of lasagna.

When he swallowed, he asked, "Are you into women now?"

I almost choked on the bite of turkey and avocado. "What? Where did that come from?"

"*You were great.* Great, not spectacular or mind blowing. If I can't please you, clearly you're into women instead," Gus replied, running his hand over his beard.

"Or you drove her away from dicks, and she now likes to dive for pussy." God, Poe was ruthless.

I looked to Gus, laughed. "No. That's not it."

"So you like dick," Gus countered.

I cleared my throat and of course, flushed hotly. "Yes."

"And you liked my dick."

"Yes."

"Good, we've established that much,"

Gus continued. "What else? You like being on top. You want to do it in my pick-up again. You like to be spanked. You want to call me Daddy. You want me to tie you up. Flog you. Fuck your ass. Eat your pussy. Play with toys. Watch you come. Go down—"

I reached out, covered Gus's mouth again, felt the soft prickle of his beard. "You don't know when to stop."

When I pull my hand away, he said, "Pixie, I can go a long, long time." Then he winked.

Kemp reached out, grabbed the sandwich from my hand. "No share, no sandwich."

I eyed him carefully. "I'm the sheriff and even I don't starve people for answers."

Glancing at Poe, he just shrugged. "You better just tell us then."

I mentally shrugged. What the hell? Gus wouldn't judge me and I didn't think Kemp or Poe would either. Worst case scenario, Gus wouldn't be interested and nothing would have changed. I hadn't *had* him in ten years.

I wanted a guy to have the same kinks as me. What better way to do that then get them out in the open right away? I didn't need to get naked and in a guy's bed to learn he couldn't—or more likely, wouldn't—do it for me. This saved a lot of time and energy getting redressed.

I glanced between the three of them who waited patiently. "I like to share, too."

A rumble came from Poe's chest.

Gus sat up straight at that, eyes filled with surprise, but eager interest. "Meaning..."

I licked my lips, looked between the three of them. "Meaning, I want to see whose dick really *is* the biggest."

4

KEMP

"With three men, you won't get vanilla," I told her.

Holy. Fucking. Shit.

She wanted all three of us. *Her.*

God, look at her. Sleek dark hair, dark eyes. Her skin was pale, but had a healthy tan from being outside. She was gorgeous in that subtle way. Not flashy. Hell, she was wearing a sheriff's uniform shirt, which had to be barely one small step up from potato sack when it came to being sexy. But she was. So fucking sexy my dick had gone harder than a fence post in two seconds flat the moment I saw her.

And she wasn't a tiny thing either. I'd worried about that whenever I'd been with a woman. I was a big guy. Big everywhere and I'd always had to be gentle. With my hands, my body, my dick.

Parker though, had to be almost six feet tall. Sturdy, lush. Strong.

Gus had talked about her, how she'd been his first, how she'd been the one who got away. But, was now back in town. He'd seen her at the family ranch, wanted her. Hoped we'd all get to have her. But it hadn't been that casual, like he'd run across his old fourth grade teacher at the grocery store. No, he'd talked about her, and talked about her some more. I'd wanted to roll my eyes for how he kept at it. How fucking gorgeous she was, how hot it had been with her, how she was even more amazing now. All that seemed a little far-fetched since he hadn't even talked with her since she'd been back. But he'd been adamant. His dick had been hard and he'd told us how often he'd had to rub one out just fantasizing about her.

That had been a lot of hoping and I'd discounted his obsession. It had been too much to wish for, a woman who'd want the three of us. Who could handle us all and he'd never said she'd go for that.

Still, he was whipped.

And now so was I. He'd been right. Every fucking word. I felt like I knew her, recognized her even though I'd never seen her before. I felt a connection, desire. Need. I needed Parker and that was fucking insane. Especially since she wanted all of us.

She stared at me now with those fathomable brown eyes. I saw heat there, wariness, too. The fact that she was brave enough to share probably her darkest, most illicit desires made me so proud of her. And I'd only just met her.

"I understand. I don't want vanilla," she replied, her voice soft. While she'd admitted to a huge truth, she'd become a little nervous.

I set down the sandwich I'd taken from her hand. "You won't be in charge with the three of us."

She'd made herself clear. It was our turn to tell her how it would be. We wanted her right there with us, so her awareness and consent were crucial.

She shook her head. "No."

Gus reached out, put his fingers to her chin and made her look at him. "You're the sheriff, pixie. Lots of responsibility. You want us to clear that head of yours."

"You want to give over, to submit, don't you?" Poe asked.

She nodded and Gus dropped his hand away. "Say it, pixie."

I watched as she licked her lips, then swallowed. "I want you to take control."

Oh fuck. I wanted to dominate her, to give her that. To make her forget everything but what we told her to do. Her job had to be stressful as fuck. Keeping the county safe, dealing with the mayor, the city council, drunks, wife beaters and worse. She needed a break, to hand off all the stress and let someone take care of her for a while.

I had no problem doing that, being that person for her. No question Poe and Gus were right there, too. I couldn't wait a second longer.

"Go over to the counter and put your hands on it," I said. While my tone was deeper than it had been before, it wasn't harsh. It made her eyes widen and yet her pupils dilated because I sank into the role and she knew things had changed.

Her cheeks turned a pretty shade of pink, which had me wondering how pink she'd be other places. Her pussy. Her nipples. Her crinkled little asshole.

"Now?" she asked, a little surprised. "Here?"

"Now," Poe replied. He'd been quiet, watching. Waiting. Until now. Now he wanted to be just as involved, for her to know that we were all in on this. Together.

I practically held my breath as we watched. It was obvious she was thinking hard. *Real* hard. It was one thing to say she wanted all of us, to have someone take charge, another to hand all that over.

Slowly, she pushed back her chair and stood. Fuck, she was gorgeous. Curvy, lush. Big. She wouldn't break because of our large hands and our big dicks. She could handle us. How she wasn't claimed yet was beyond me. And yet, she wasn't a virgin. Some idiot let her go, which was our gain.

She walked over to the counter, set her hands on the flat surface just as I'd asked. Her back was to us, so she glanced over her shoulder. Wariness and heat. Her teeth sunk into her bottom lip. "This is a little weird. I haven't seen Gus in years and I've just met you two."

Poe pushed his chair back, turned it so we faced her. Had a front row seat to a sexy show.

"There's not much difference between right now and tonight," I said.

We'd wait, no problem. If she wasn't comfortable or ready, we'd give her all the time in the world. But she'd done exactly as I'd said. She wanted this, even if her mind was struggling with it.

VANESSA VALE

"I feel like one of you is going to frisk me or something."

"Only if you want us to," I replied.

"I'm working."

"And we will be soon, too," Gus added. "Trust us. Give over, pixie."

She took a deep breath, let it out. Nodded.

Fuck, yes. "All I want you to do right now is work your jeans down over your hips, stick that gorgeous ass out and show us your pussy," I told her. "We'll sit right here and watch."

Her mouth fell open, but she didn't look like she wanted to come across the room and slap me, or worse, use her Taser on me. No, her cheeks flushed even darker and she bit her lip. Her mind was working. Hard. But she was aroused. Interested. Willing.

"I thought you were going to show me which of you has the biggest dick."

"Later," Gus said. He did a little

circle with his finger as a silent command to turn around.

We waited. Gus had barely moved since she'd stood up, clearly a little stunned how things were going. He'd hoped she'd be into all three of us, but probably expected to have to woo her, court her even, coax her into the idea.

There'd been no coaxing. Hell no.

She might not have been so bold on her own, but that didn't mean she didn't want to have three men watch her. Since I told her what to do, commanded even, it had taken the pressure off her shoulders. I was *making* her show us her pussy, which made it okay for her. She was submitting to my words, doing as I wanted, which in turn, got her exactly what she needed.

She turned away once again, worked the belt on her jeans and shimmied them down her legs so they settled mid-thigh. The creamy skin was just a small strip because her shirttail fell over her ass. With her utility belt snug around her waist, loaded with her gun, Taser, cuffs and other things, she couldn't pull it up. Still, the fact that she'd done what I'd said made pre-cum drip from my dick. I shifted in my chair trying to get comfortable.

Parker was submissive. An exhibitionist, at least to a degree. She'd show herself to us, but no one else. She wasn't shy. Wasn't timid in her sexuality. And, she was horny. For all three of us.

"Stick that ass out, pixie," Gus told her. He ran a hand over the back of his neck, as if he were struggling not to go over and tug her hips back for her. To open up his jeans, pull out his dick and fuck her.

I knew the feeling.

Lowering herself to her forearms, Parker bent over and that had her shirt riding up, her ass exposed, but cover in silky pink panties. The gusset was darker, wet from her arousal and the material clung to her folds.

"Oh shit," Gus whispered, and out of the corner of my eye—no fucking way was I looking away from Parker—saw him shift himself in his jeans.

She wasn't looking at us, but straight at the wall in front of her.

He hopped to his feet, moved closer. She glanced up at him in surprise, but remained in position.

"You like it when three men look at you," he said. As if it were too painful otherwise, he opened his jeans, reached in and pulled out his dick. It was hard as a rock and pre-cum dripped from the slit. When Parker licked her lips, I knew she hadn't missed his obvious need for her.

Gus's jaw clenched as he stroked his length, slow at first then faster.

VANESSA VALE

"That silk's soaked. We can see every bit of your pussy lips, how hard your clit is."

He reached out, ran a finger over the gusset of her panties. Her hips bucked but she remained in place. She gasped and I groaned.

"Fuck, I'm going to come just seeing that little birth mark again. I want to get between those thighs and kiss it." He breathed deep as he worked his dick. "Fuck, I can smell your pussy all hot and sugary from here."

"Gus," she moaned, wiggling her hips, wanting him to do more. Fuck yes.

That was all it took and Gus came on a growl. "Fuck, pixie."

His cum spurted from him and he moved so it landed on her upturned ass, stained her panties.

She looked up at him again, now with hooded eyes, flushed cheeks. "Are you going to fuck me now?"

70

"You want that, don't you?" he asked, pumping the last of the cum from his balls. "To be fucked in front of Poe and Kemp? To let them see how needy your pussy is?"

She nodded. Oh shit, she was so fucking perfect. Upturned ass, Gus's cum in stripes across it, soaked panties, pussy lips outlined. I was going to come in my jeans.

"Can't, pixie. There's no time for what we want to do to you. With three men fucking you, a lunch quickie won't do it. We all have to get back to work. Besides, we don't have any condoms."

She whimpered, wiggled some more as if it would bring friction to her clit.

I had my hand on my dick over my jeans, rubbing it, trying to ease the ache, but I knew it wouldn't go away until I was balls deep in that hot pussy.

"Take those soaked panties down," he added. "Show us how wet you are for all three of us. Then you'll work your clit and we'll watch you come."

She shifted with eagerness to get off and began to push the skimpy fabric off her hips, then lower. The silk clung to her pussy from all that sticky arousal. Before we could see more than her pale, upturned ass, the radio on her hip beeped once, then again, and a dispatcher's voice shut down our little show. She had new orders, and they weren't from the three of us.

Fuck.

5

POE

"It figures," I grumbled, leaning against the counter in the small lab we had between patient rooms. I'd just finished with a German Shepherd with mild hip dysplasia. Kemp was looking at a slide under a microscope for worms. Gus had a lull between appointments and was drinking a cup of coffee. "The woman of my dreams, the one who'd said she wanted all three of us, the one you shot your load all over, who *almost* showed us her pussy, is a fucking cop."

Kemp glanced up at me and grinned. "So? What does that have to do with anything but her being totally into all of us, and having handcuffs readily available?"

That was a definite perk, but not the point. "It doesn't bother you she was bent over the counter showing us her wet panties, getting off on having Gus jack off all over her, then had to go on a call?"

They stared at me with a look I recognized. They thought I was crazy.

"She's the sheriff. She responds to emergencies," Gus replied. "It's not like she planned to tease us with seeing her pussy then run out the door. She left all hot and bothered."

That was a total cock tease—knowing she was out there somewhere horny as hell and with Gus's cum all over her panties. My balls ached because of it. It wasn't that though. They still didn't get it.

"Yeah, but people are idiots. *Dangerous* idiots. I don't care if it's her job. Doesn't mean I have to like it," I told him.

Gus pinned me with a serious stare. "She's not going to care about your past. If that's what you're worried about."

I waved off his words. "Care about my stint in juvie? That isn't my problem."

"Then what's got your panties in a twist?" Kemp asked, turning the focus dial and looking down the lens.

"She shouldn't be out there, dealing with the fuck ups of society." I lifted my arm, waved it in the air. "I know them. I was one of them."

"You were not," Kemp replied. "You saved your mom from your abusive father. You were defending her. You did the right thing."

I ran my hand through my hair. I needed a haircut, but that wasn't very high on my list. Maybe this winter I'd grow a beard like Gus. Less maintenance than shaving every damn day, but I had to wonder if that was something Parker would like. "Still, she doesn't need to see that shit, let alone deal with it. She might get hurt."

Kemp and Gus were protective fuckers, took care of what was theirs. *Who* was theirs. Especially women. Sure, they hadn't liked her *almost* sharing her pink, wet pussy with us and then tugging up her jeans and running out the door, the stray dog hot on her heels. But why it didn't bother them that Parker had to leave us for a domestic dispute call, I had no idea. Well, maybe I did.

There was no fucking way Mr. Duke

would lay a hand on his wife in anger. He cherished the fuck out of that woman and he'd raised all three of his sons, Gus, Tucker and Duke, to not only be gentlemen, but to do what was right. Protect. I had no idea how their little sister, Julia, would ever find a man with three older brothers watching out for her.

As for Kemp, I'd only met his parents once since they lived in Minnesota, but his dad wouldn't stand for any of that shit either.

But I'd grown up with a bastard for a dad. Mean. Cruel. And I'd killed him because of it. But knowing Parker had gone—as part of her job—to confront someone as possibly fucked up as my dad made me restless, made me want to chase after her, deal with the problem myself.

"She doesn't go into shit alone. She's got backup," Gus said. "Look, I'm not wild about it either, but this is her job, what she wants to do. She's smart. She's trained. You're going to have to deal at least until election day. Right now, it's Hogan versus Beirstad."

"Yeah, Beirstad. What a prick. Isn't his brother the one who fucked with Kaitlyn?"

"That's the one," Gus said. I'd heard about the confrontation at Cassidy's and that he was leaving Kaitlyn alone now, but that didn't make him any less an asshole. I didn't know much about the guy, but his brother, Mark, was just as bad from what I'd heard.

"The city council felt she was qualified and she seems to be doing a good job."

He was right, but that didn't mean I had to like any of it. Let Hogan and Beirstad deal with the meth heads and wife beaters. Raines was a peaceful town, but that didn't mean everything was rainbows and sunshine. "Why can't she have a job like Kaitlyn? The only danger she faces at the library is a paper cut."

Why couldn't my dick get hard for a woman who had a safe career? Why did one look at Parker ruin me for all other women? And that was before she'd submitted to Kemp and had been ready to show us her pussy. Begged for us to fuck her in the office kitchen. FUCK!

"I'm not doubting Parker's qualifications to be sheriff or that she can take care of herself, but like I said, that doesn't mean I have to like it."

Gus shrugged and couldn't help but smile. He'd told us about Parker Drew and her return to town. His mom was on the city council and among those who'd voted to hire her, so there was no doubt she'd tossed that little bomb at him since she wanted all her kids happily married—and at least practicing on making her some grandbabies. Maybe Mrs. Duke was hoping for a little second chance romance.

Second chance fucking, definitely. After lunch today, hopefully soon.

Parker—as sheriff—had had to go to the Duke ranch and deal with some loser and Gus had seen her, wanted her. Decided she'd be the one for the three of us. Hoped we'd agree.

Abso-fucking-lutely should she be the one for us. What were the chances a woman wanted to take on three men? Kaitlyn and Ava decided to wrangle two guys each, but three? The hopes of finding a woman willing to do that were slim. That was, until Parker had walked into the office kitchen and I'd vowed then and there I'd do anything to get her to want us.

She was The One. No question.

And then she'd changed everything

with the words *I want to see whose dick really is the biggest.* There was no way to misconstrue that. She *wanted* to be with the three of us.

I shifted my dick, trying to find a way to keep from getting a zipper imprint in it.

And then she'd gone even further, submitting to Kemp. Fuck, I'd been hard ever since seeing her perfect ass, watching her hips shift with need, the dark spot on her panties grow as Gus talked dirty to her. I was definitely an ass man. I'd envisioned getting a grip on those wide hips as I fucked her from behind. Or seeing pink handprints where I spanked her into forgetting about her crazy day. Or parting those full cheeks and getting into that tight ass. Stretching her open and taking her deep. That left two other holes for Gus and Kemp.

Ever since lunch, since Parker got

that fucking call, pulled up her pants and left, the two of them couldn't stop smiling. I could understand Gus since he'd busted a nut all over her ass, but Kemp should have a serious case of blue balls. I did. And the very idea of the three of us claiming her at once? I'd forced myself to will my dick into submission while I worked and tried not to think about the heaven she'd almost shown us. That wasn't working so well.

"A gorgeous woman is coming over tonight to continue where we left off, most likely to fuck all three of us and you're grumbling and complaining like a crochety old man," Kemp said as he tossed the slide into the sharps container, tugged off his rubber gloves and washed his hands in the sink.

I perked up at his words. "She's coming over?"

"Have you checked your phone

lately?" Gus asked, pulling his from the back pocket of his jeans and waving it back and forth. "I got her cell number, remember?"

"I was dealing with Mr. Bracco's geriatric cat, followed by Charlie the Shepherd, then a parrot who lost a toenail," I replied as way of recapping my busy afternoon, completely forgetting he'd snagged her number before she ran out.

"I thought I heard a bird," Gus said as I retrieved my cell, swiped the screen.

*G*us: *Come over after work. We'll take care of your needy pussy.*

I noted he'd sent it right after she left.

. . .

Parker: OK

Her response was timed much later—in fact, just ten minutes ago—I assumed after the call she'd left us to attend. At least I knew she was okay, thank fuck. Raines wasn't known for a shit ton of crime, but bad things could happen anywhere.

Then Kemp had chimed in on the group text.

Kemp: Since you had your panties halfway down, clothes are optional.
Parker: I should come naked?

• • •

"*H*oly shit," I muttered, thinking of her showing up in just a trench coat and fuck-me heels.

Out of the corner of my eye, I saw Gus grin and tip up his chin toward me. "Send her something so she knows we're all into this."

"She's the fucking sheriff," I countered.

"Yeah, and if you get your head out of your ass, you'll be fucking the sheriff all night long," Kemp added, drying his hands.

Since he was annoying, but accurate, I paused, thought of what to type.

*M*e: We can make you come dressed, naked, riding any one of our dicks. Even two of them.

• • •

I hit send and both of their cells vibrated. Gus looked at his. "Nice." Then he typed as fast as his big thumbs would allow.

*M*y cell vibrated—we didn't leave the ringers on during working hours—and I read his addition.

*G*us: *That's right, pixie. You can have all three of us at the same time if you want. And I promise, you'll come.*

*H*er response came almost immediately.

. . .

Parker: I need it. Bad. I get off at six.

"My turn," Kemp said, then typed.

"I don't think I've ever felt more like a thirteen-year-old girl," I muttered, glancing at Gus. He grinned in response, not the least bit fazed by my statement. We were group texting a girl. Yeah, we were totally pussy whipped. After her perfect display of submission and how naughty she was, no guy could blame us.

Kemp: With the three of us taking care of you, you'll get off all night long.

Parker: Just so you know, it's your fault I'm meeting the mayor with ruined panties.

*A*nd that was it. I was done for. I could imagine her sitting in the mayor's office squirming because of Gus's cum and the fact that her panties were soaked with pussy juice. I remembered the pretty pink color, the fact that they'd been so wet as to be transparent, all because of us. I pressed my palm against my dick, then looked at the time. "In just a minute, I've got a litter of puppies for their first shots in room two. You have to cover me for a few."

"Where are you going?" Kemp asked, one eyebrow shifting up under his curly hair.

I tilted my head. "Bathroom. I've got to rub one out. I can't go in there like this."

Both of them glanced at the front of my jeans. My dick was like a thick pipe angling up to my belt. If I leaned forward, the tip would probably come out of the waistband.

"That was me an hour ago." Kemp walked past me, slapped me on the shoulder on the way. "Have fun. Think of Parker and her dripping pussy."

6

PARKER

"*Y*ou look great," Gus said when he opened the door for me.

He paused and glanced down because the dog trotted in behind me as if she were invited, too.

"I see you've still got your sidekick," he commented as she sat down and stared up at him. He petted the top of her head and scratched a spot behind her ear which had her eyes falling closed as if she were in heaven. I knew that feeling well; I used to love having Gus's hands on me.

I was strangely jealous of a dog.

"When I got the call earlier, she followed me to the SUV, climbed in through the driver's side and settled in the passenger seat. I couldn't waste any time kicking her out, so she came along for the ride. Pam at the station went out and got her a bag of food, a dog bed and some toys. You'd think she has a new grandchild or something." I rolled my eyes at how excited everyone at the station had been to have a dog around. "I brought her here to pawn her off on you. Her stuff's in the SUV. I'm not really a dog person."

"Doesn't look that way to me," he countered, glancing my way and *finally* ignoring the dog. "I think she's yours now."

I wasn't too thrilled about that idea. "I have a full time job. Stuff to do. I don't know anything about having a dog."

Gus smiled and tucked his hands into his jeans pockets. "Looks like you're doing okay so far."

The dog's nose twitched and she went in search of some smell I couldn't detect.

Without the distraction, Gus turned his full attention back to me, took his time to look me over.

After work, I'd gone home to shower, put on something a little more attractive than the sheriff's uniform and a utility belt with a gun on my hip. I didn't want to be the sheriff for them. Hell, I was for everyone else in town. That's how the people of Raines knew me, at least these days. Maybe some remembered me from growing up, but I was Sheriff Drew now. I just wanted to be Parker. Nothing more, especially for Gus, Kemp and Poe.

I'd stood in front of my closet for fifteen minutes debating. While sleeping with them—okay, sex—was a sure thing at this point, I wanted them to be a little more than attracted to me. I wanted Gus to be like he had been earlier, so turned on he'd come by hardly touching me. I wanted to not only look nice for them, but to feel good about myself as well. I wanted to know *I*, unexciting Sheriff Parker, could entice three hot vets.

At the same time, I had no intention of overdoing it. I wanted them to know the real me, and that included fresh jeans, a red flannel shirt and sexy underwear. I had my hair down and wore a little makeup—mascara, eyeliner and lip gloss were all I could ever accomplish.

At Gus's heated appreciation as he

took me in, it seemed I'd chosen well, that his dick was thick in his jeans for me and me alone.

I'd been so worked up when I'd gotten the call earlier. Still was. To say I was horny was an understatement. There was no way Kemp could have known an emergency would have interrupted us, but it had been almost mean to be so turned on, then left to ache all day. I hadn't lied when I texted them about how wet my panties were.

Even though he'd been the only one who'd come, it was reassuring to know Gus was—once again? Still?—just as... eager as I.

Kemp joined us in the entryway. Both wore worn-in jeans, molded oh-so-well to all the right places. Firm butts, muscular thighs, ridiculously large dicks. Kemp had on a plaid flannel shirt, Gus a black t-shirt. Both were barefooted. God, even their feet were sexy.

"Your dog's staring at the fish tank," Kemp said, thumbing over his shoulder, but he had his eyes on me. On my lips, specifically.

"She's not my dog," I countered.

"I think she disagrees. You should name her. It'll make it easier for all of us."

I rolled my eyes. "Fine. Buster. Daisy. Spot."

Kemp stepped closer, ran his fingers along the edge of my hair. His attention was focused there as he responded. "How about Honey? She's well trained. A sweet dog, but probably not as sweet as your pussy. My mouth's watering to get a taste."

Heat flared low in my belly, but all of a sudden, I thought about what we were going to do. I'd fantasized about being with more than one man, masturbated to it. Recognized I needed it. But it had been just that, a fantasy. Now, it was really going to happen.

I got nervous, butterflies in my belly. My nerves must have showed, because he added, "You look like a wild mustang ready to bolt."

Gus grinned as he closed the front door, took my hand and led me into the huge great room. I hoped he couldn't tell my palms were sweaty. White walls, stained wood trim and floors. Thick beams in the ceiling. Leather furniture and a two-story stone fireplace. It was big, just like they were.

Kemp followed and Poe joined us, coming from a back hallway. He nodded, tucked his hands in the front pockets of his jeans. God, I'd forgotten how big he was; I had to look up at him. *A lot.*

"Hey," he said, his voice deep and smooth. His intense stare made me feel naked. Exposed. As if he were holding himself back from… pouncing.

The dog… Honey, was sitting in front of a huge salt water tank. She turned her head to glance at me, but wasn't all that interested and returned her attention to the bright fish swimming about.

She wasn't nervous. I was. *Really* nervous. Lunch with them had been insane. Crazy! And I hadn't even had anything to eat to really call it *lunch*. Not only had I told three men—two who I'd never even met before—that I wanted to sleep with them… together, but I'd actually bent over their office kitchen's counter and shown them my butt. And Gus…god, that had been hot. He'd been too worked up to leave his dick in his pants. My panties had been sticky all day from the cum he'd shot all over the back of the pink fabric.

If I hadn't gotten that call and run

out, I'd have shown them even more. No question. My fingers had been working my panties down when we'd been interrupted. I'd been wet then, and just from the way they'd looked at me, the way they told me what to do. The idea of three men... god, dominating me, handling me roughly, touching me with a fevered need so my busy mind could just shut up had made me so hot. Horny.

I'd been so turned on I'd have let them fuck me, too.

I was *so* not that kind of girl. Well, I was. Partly. I wanted to sleep with Gus, Kemp *and* Poe, wanted to listen to Kemp's deep voice and do what he said, get under Gus again and let Poe handle me with those big hands—and most likely equally big dick—but I'd never done something so naughty within a few minutes of meeting someone.

But I knew Gus. Remembered how

it had been and wanted more with him. As for Kemp and Poe, it was ridiculous, but I just *knew*. I felt the connection, the instant desire, interest and curiosity right away. Trust was required and that had taken time with guys in the past. Lots of it. I always needed a long getting-to-know-you period before I let someone tie me up or even be verbally dominant. I had to be in the right headspace, and I couldn't do that with someone I didn't trust implicitly.

How I could do that with these three... immediately, was what was a little overwhelming.

It meant something. *This* meant something. Something big that I couldn't think about right now.

All I knew was that I'd been turned on all day, even in the meeting with the mayor. Honey had followed me around the station and into the meeting. It wasn't every day a dog tagged along and it was a good thing people in Raines were laid back. Thankfully, she'd distracted him enough to miss that I was squirming in my chair.

And the texts they'd sent. Holy shit. All three of them had written, promising I'd come, and had kept my need simmering all day.

"We won't bite. Not unless you want us to," Kemp offered.

I huffed out a small laugh combined with a harsh exhale. "Sorry, you're right, I am nervous," I told him, but my mind was stuck on the idea of him actually biting me. A little nibble, his teeth scraping across the tip of my nipple. I clenched my core at the thought and my nipples were hard tips pressing against my bra.

Kemp's curly hair was slightly damp, as if he'd just gotten out of the shower. I took a deep breath to calm my racing heart and got a whiff of a woodsy scent.

Soap of some kind. Dark and manly. He hadn't shaved though, light whiskers covered his square jaw. His easy smile had little wrinkles form by his eyes. I could read people—a skill I'd learned really well working in the District Attorney's office and dealing with clients who weren't as innocent as they seemed, then honed during police academy—and it showed he was easy going. Laid back. Yet he seemed to be the most dominant one of the trio.

"You? Nervous? After what you did earlier?" Gus commented, coming close enough to stroke a big hand down my hair.

"What I did? What about you?" I countered. "You're the one who got to come."

He only grinned in reply, his white teeth in stark contrast to his dark beard.

I felt my cheeks heat. "Still," I replied, remembering how I'd gotten wetter and wetter and I'd been hot all over as I'd felt their eyes on me, knew they could see how eager I'd been.

Now, they stepped close, surrounded me. I'd taken in the house when I'd parked, walked up to the front door. Modern log cabin would be the term. Rustic Montana but with huge windows to take in the views. It was a big house for big men. I knew they lived together and this place suited. But they weren't going to take me on a tour.

All I could see, feel, breathe was Gus, Poe and Kemp. Big men. Surrounding.

"I'd have never done that if you hadn't told me to," I admitted.

Kemp lifted my chin with his finger and I met his eyes. I hadn't realized I'd been staring at his flannel shirt until then. "You told us what you wanted. That you wanted all three of us. That you wanted us to take control. That was enough. We did… and will take it from there."

These words were softly spoken, completely unlike that pussy-wetting tone he'd used that had gotten my pants down.

"Even nervous, you came here. Very brave to take what you want," Poe said, and I turned my head to look at him. Dark, potent, with eyes so surprisingly pale they matched his intensity. All his focus was on me and it was like being touched. Caressed. In thrall, and he hadn't laid even a finger on me. Not once. "We couldn't miss how wet your pussy was earlier. When you got home from work, did you make yourself come to ease the ache?"

I shook my head.

"You didn't lie back on your bed, spread your thighs and play?" Gus asked.

"No," I whispered. I'd wanted to. My

clit had throbbed, my pussy needy through my shift. My nipples had chafed against my bra, and yet I hadn't pulled out my vibrator like I'd wanted. I'd had three hot guys to fill my mind to help me come, but I'd held off.

I'd wanted the real thing. Standing between them now, I was glad I had.

"Good girl," Gus added. "That pussy belongs to us. Those orgasms are ours. No touching without us or you'll be punished."

I swallowed at his words and my pussy heated. *Punished.*

The 9-1-1 call that had come in when I'd been busy pulling my jeans down for them had been a domestic disturbance. One where the wife had obviously been abused by her husband. He'd answered the door with a wicked grin that proved this had happened before, that he knew he would get away with it. He had, too, because his wife, with bruises on top of fading bruises, had refused to press charges. Her calling for help in the first place was the obvious sign that her man had taken control and "changed her mind" for her. God, it had bothered me. Still did, knowing she was at home with that fucker right now. But, she was a grown woman and unless she chose to have him arrested, there would be nothing I could do. At least not today.

And because Gus had said the word *punished*, it instantly flared my anger, but it quickly died out. He wouldn't hurt me. Ever.

"What's that look, pixie?" he asked. Yeah, he could read me. Always had. After ten years of being apart, it felt good. Familiar.

I told him about the call and the three of them looked furious. It definitely only helped confirm my decision not to put my name on the ballot for the job. I was a temporary sheriff and nothing more. I'd rather work back in a DA's office and ensure people like that asshole never get out of jail. I'd talked to Porter Duke, the county DA and, coincidentally, Gus's cousin, about a job in that office. The position was waiting for me in November, which was reassuring, allowing me to stay in town near Momma... and now possibly three huge men.

Poe swore under his breath. "That's not us, Parker," he vowed. "And if you tell us this guy's name, we'll make sure he's taken care of."

I looked to Poe, smiled. For someone so big, he was really sweet. Ruthlessly intent and I had no doubt he would take care of the asshole without breaking a sweat, but still, sweet. "That isn't something you want to tell the sheriff," I replied.

"He hurts a woman, he deserves what he gets," he countered in a harsh snarl, then walked off, raking his hand through his black hair as he went. Clearly, this was a touchy subject for him.

"You know what we're doing here is different, right?" Kemp asked, turning my attention back to him. "That when Gus said we'd punish you, it would be more *funishment*. All you'll get from us is pleasure… eventually."

Yeah, that one word went against every feminist bone in my body. Why wasn't I kneeing him in the balls and telling him I could take care of myself, including my pleasure? Why did I have to give a man—or men—control? Why did I *want* them to have it?

"That asshole *took* control from his wife, pixie," Gus said, brushing a knuckle down my cheek. "You're *giving* it to us. A gift. And we'll keep it safe. And you."

"You call the shots," Kemp added. "All of them. At the clinic, I told you to bend over and show us that gorgeous ass. You did it because you wanted to, no other reason. You could have said no, hell, said pineapple as a safe word and we'd have respected that."

"That's right, pixie," Gus added, eyes narrowing at Kemp, probably about the word pineapple, which had come out of nowhere. "As you can see, we want you between us. But only if you want to be there."

I was between the two of them right now and it was *exactly* the place for me. I wanted to be surrounded, overwhelmed, even overpowered. *Especially* after the call from earlier. I wanted to do nothing more than forget about it. About everything.

"We have to learn how far to push

you, what makes you hot and wet. Nothing further."

I gave Kemp a little nod. He seemed to be the most dominant of the trio, that his nature was a little more commanding.

"Back to what I said," Gus replied. "We're in charge of that pussy until you say otherwise. Every inch of you when we're like this. Obey or that ass is going to be well-spanked."

"Or we'll plug your ass," Kemp added.

"Or tie you to the bed and deny you orgasms," Gus finished.

All of that made me squirm. I'd been spanked before, even did some butt stuff. Orgasm denial sounded miserable though, because I'd been living that all day long. I was sure they could make me come so hard, but my pussy clenched in response nonetheless. My brain might be thinking one thing, but the rest of me was right there with these guys. This was play. While they were in charge, I was the one with all the say.

I'd wanted them to get me out of my head, so I had to make my brain shut the fuck up. Spanked, plugged, deliciously tortured. It made me melt. It made me wet. It made me say, "Yes, sir."

"Oh fuck," Kemp whispered, then wrapped an arm about my waist and gently pulled me into him so his front was to my back. I felt every hard, hot inch of him. And by that, I meant not only his chest and sturdy thighs, but the long, thick feel of his dick pressing into my ass. He kissed the side of my neck and my eyes fell closed. "How are you so perfect?"

I smiled. "Far from it. You don't really know me."

"I know this spot right here tastes like hot sugar." He licked my neck then gave it a gentle grazing with his teeth. Gentle, but with a hint of bite. Literally. Goose bumps rose on my skin and I whimpered.

His hand spanned my entire belly, the tips of his fingers brushed the underside of my breasts. It showed how big Kemp was, because I wasn't a small woman.

"I bet the rest of you tastes just as sweet," he continued. "Especially that sticky honey between your thighs."

Kemp was a dirty talker, which also made him a panty-ruiner because I was soaked.

"I remember," Gus said. "Like candy."

Kemp groaned and I felt the rumble at my back.

"We want to know all about you," Gus continued. "In bed and out."

His thumb settled on my lower lip and I opened my eyes. I looked to him, saw the dark gaze I remembered. I parted my lips and the tip slipped in. I sucked on his thumb, swirled my tongue around. Watched his jaw clench, his eyes turn black from the need. I'd sucked his dick a long time ago. I hadn't been very good at it, more eagerness than skill, but I remembered. How big he'd been in my mouth, how much I'd had to open my mouth to get him to fit. His taste, the hot, velvety yet hard feel against my tongue.

And it seemed he remembered, too.

"If you keep doing that, we won't make it to a bed this first time," Kemp offered, taking my hand and placing it over the front of his pants so I couldn't miss how hard he was. And big. So big, he may have been right when he said Gus was the smallest.

He was ready. Right now. My nerves were gone. Wiped away along with most of my thoughts. Kemp's mouth on my neck. Gus's thumb in my mouth. Poe was around here somewhere.

"We're going to have to be very careful with you, pixie," Gus murmured. "We're the ones in charge and yet you're going to bring me to my knees with just that hot mouth of yours."

He pulled his thumb free and stepped back. Kemp's arm about me tightened, held me against him, a reminder I'd handed over my power. Gus eyed me.

"Ready, Parker?" Kemp asked. I couldn't see his face, but the deep timbre of his voice was laced with blatant need.

I nodded, my head bumping his shoulder.

"We need to hear it," Gus added.

I swallowed. This was it, the verbal consent they wanted to play and play wild.

"Yes."

Kemp turned me to face him, then arched a pale brow. "Yes, what?"

I shivered. "Yes, sir."

He smiled, all dark and full of heat. Promise.

7

GUS

*K*emp had been right. The hot, wet suction of her mouth on the tip of my thumb had pre-cum practically dripping from my dick. If I looked down, no doubt a wet patch was growing bigger on the front of my jeans. But I wasn't tearing my gaze away from Parker. And I had plenty of cum to get in her. Sure, I'd been like a teenager and spurted all over her upturned ass. But I'd stayed hard, stored up the rest of my cum for her pussy. Or her mouth. Maybe even her ass.

While Kemp and Poe had rubbed one out at the office, I hadn't come again. It might not have been the best idea, for once I got in her, the way I felt right now I'd pump a few times and be done.

It was all her fault, coming here looking all fuck-me perfect. The sweet, eager teenager I remembered, but better. More beautiful. Wiser. So fucking sexy. She must have gone home to change because while she still wore jeans, the uniform shirt was gone. In its place was a red flannel, the top two buttons undone. Nothing flashy, nothing overly feminine or high maintenance, which totally worked for me.

With the shirt tucked in, no one

could miss she was *all* woman with her hourglass figure. She was more than a handful. Everywhere. And I loved that. I wasn't small, hell, I towered over most women. But not her. I had a few inches on her, but I never had to bend in half to kiss her. And when she was beneath me and I was fucking her, I remembered how easy it had been to reach her mouth with mine, even those ample breasts. And fuck, did I want to see them again. I wanted to rip the buttons off her shirt to see those large nipples I'd sucked so fondly. To watch as they hardened in the cooler air, against my tongue.

Shit. I couldn't remember a time my dick was so hard. I'd need Parker to help me with the problem because I refused to finish like I had earlier.

I took her hand and led her upstairs to my bedroom, Kemp right there with us.

Poe had walked off after hearing about the call, about the guy beating his wife. I didn't blame him for taking a minute, that kind of situation always messed with him because of his mom. But he had to get his shit together and join us or he'd be missing out. Kemp and I could satisfy Parker, no question. But she wanted all of us and we'd give her anything her fucking heart desired. Especially if it were three dicks.

I led her to the foot of my big bed. Kemp's and Poe's rooms were down the hall. While we'd share her, we'd have to take turns sleeping with her at night. Yes, I was thinking of forever. I remembered what we had, what we'd walked away from. Not again.

But adding Kemp and Poe obviously changed the dynamic. It wasn't as if we wanted this huge-ass bed the four of us could sleep in together. That was fucking weird.

Didn't mean the three of us wouldn't fuck her together though. Starting right now.

"Kemp's going to get you undressed, pixie."

I stepped away, dropped into the overstuffed chair by the window where I usually read before bed. Parker looked a little surprised I'd moved away from her, but I had her attention. Especially when I did some manspreading, opened up my jeans, pushed them down enough to get my dick out. It was so fucking hard I hissed when I gripped the base. I'd never seen it so angry looking, the color a dark plum, so full of blood the vein that ran up the length pulsed and bulged. The crown glistened with pre-cum. And I'd come all over her hours ago.

"This is all because of you," I told her. "I'm going to sit here and stroke my dick and watch you with Kemp. My own little strip show. You're too fucking gorgeous for my dick to handle. I need to come again to take the edge off and then I can go at you all night."

She licked her lips as she watched my fist slide up and down. Kemp turned her head, redirecting her attention and kissed her.

Fuck.

This wasn't a gentle, friendly peck either, but a devouring. A dominant first kiss. His tongue was deep in her mouth as one of his hands settled on her ass, pulling her in close, the other tangled in her hair, tugging. I could hear her whimper, watch the moment she gave over, her body going lax in his hold.

Finally, they came up for air.

"Kemp, please," she begged, her voice soft, escaping on little pants.

"Today's been rough, hasn't it, baby girl? All worked up by your three men, then called away. And you have come. Your pussy must be aching for dick."

She nodded.

Kemp gave her a gentle push so she sat on the edge of the bed, then dropped to his knees before her. He worked off one of her boots, then the other before working at her jeans. He had her bare from the waist down in record time—Parker was certainly eager to lift her hips and help—with her pants and panties a pile on the carpet.

Through all this, I stroked and watched. My own personal porno with the leading lady being the woman of my dreams.

Kemp pushed her knees wide and his gaze fixed between. I remembered what she looked like there. At eighteen, she'd had the dark hair neatly trimmed, her inner lips large enough to part her slit, her clit hard and right... fucking... there.

Kemp licked his lips and leaned in. With his big hands on her inner thighs, she wasn't going anywhere, not that she was resisting in any way.

Her eyes closed and her head fell back at the first touch of his mouth. "Kemp!" she cried.

Fuck, that sound, the need in it made me spurt pre-cum all over my fist. I remembered her taste and my mouth watered for that sweet flavor again. The scent of her all over my face.

"Holy fuck," Poe said as he came in the room, a big box of condoms in his hand. Smart. We'd work our way through all of them tonight.

I was glad he'd pulled his shit together and was ready to play.

Parker looked to him, her eyes a blurry haze of pleasure. She stiffened slightly, probably realizing three men were seeing her get eaten out—her mind got distracted—but Kemp slipped his hand between her thighs and I knew the second a finger or two slid inside her.

"Grab a leg and get her nice and open for me," Kemp told him, his voice the deepest I'd ever heard it. He barely lifted his mouth from her pussy. "Baby girl's been so good, saving her pleasure all day just for us."

"Gladly." Poe went over to the bed, dropped the box of condoms and put a hand on one of her bare knees and pushed it wide and toward her chest. Parker fell back onto the soft bed and I could see so much more. Glimpses of the pinkest pussy, so wet Kemp had a lot of work to do to clean her up.

My balls drew up and I could feel the orgasm building at the base of my spine. Just from watching. Again.

"Is Kemp giving you what you

need?" Poe asked, looking down at our girl.

"Yes!" she cried, writhing as much as she could with them holding her so securely.

"Gus, get over here and hold her other knee," Kemp ordered.

While I didn't want to let go of my dick, I did want to watch as Parker came, up close. Pushing out of the chair, I joined them, taking her other knee and opening her up. I left my pants open; there was no way my dick was fitting back in until I came a few times. She was so wide Poe and I could watch as Kemp ate her out. He lifted his head for a second, let us get a look at her.

Before I took in her open pussy, I leaned down, kissed her. Met her dark eyes. "Hey, Pixie. Time to come."

She nodded, licked her lips. She was right there, so close and it hadn't even been much more than a minute. She'd been primed all day. The taste of her lips, the hot scent of her arousal had me groaning. I moved so I could look at her.

"Oh fuck, such a pretty pussy." And it was. All pink and open, her lower lips parted so we could see everything. Her opening clenched, as if it were trying to find a dick to pull inside. And she was dripping wet, even after Kemp made some effort to lick it all up. Her thighs were glistening and so was Kemp's mouth. Even the little pink asshole, all coated in her juices, winked at us.

"And sweet. I was right, she's sweeter than honey," Kemp told us.

I had no idea how she had the brain function to reach out and grab my dick, but she did. Her little fist gripped it, stroked it once and that was all it took. I came, my hips thrusting toward her. Cum shot from me like a fountain, thick spurts of it landing on her inner thighs, sliding down toward her pussy. Fortunately, Kemp had lifted his head. White hot pleasure sizzled my brain, made my muscles tense, then weak. I groaned through the blinding pleasure. And all she'd done was touch me. I was no better than when I was eighteen.

When I could open my eyes, I looked down at her. She had a satisfied smile on her face, even though she was the one who'd not yet come.

"Oh, you think you're in charge?" I asked, trying to catch my breath.

"You came, didn't you?" she countered.

Poe's hand came down on her ass with a light crack. She startled, but couldn't move much. No, we had her held down. Opened wide.

He tsked her. "Sweetheart, sass gets you spanked."

My dick was still hard; it wasn't going down anytime soon, especially seeing Poe's handprint blooming on her pale skin. But thank fuck, my mind wasn't clouded by the driving need to come. Now I could focus on her. We had all night and with three men, she was going to leave for work in the morning well-satisfied. I doubted she'd be able to walk right.

"Kemp, our girl's too in her head," Poe said.

"You're right," Kemp replied. He looked up at Parker from between her thighs. "Gus and Poe are holding you down, baby girl. This pussy's ours. Maybe I should tease this hard little clit for a while."

He leaned down, flicked the hard pearl with the tip of his tongue. She thrashed her head back and forth.

"No, I'm sorry. I'll be good."

I couldn't help but grin at the desperate pout to her voice.

"There's nothing you can do but

come," he told her.

She moaned, let her head fall back as Kemp got busy.

She wanted us to take control. Oh, we would.

8

PARKER

*O*h. My. God. Kemp had a wicked, ruthless tongue. It wasn't easy sometimes to let go enough for a guy to make me come. My mind would be too distracted. Something. Too many possibilities. But now, Poe and Gus held me down, my legs spread so wide I couldn't hide. I couldn't do anything but feel Kemp's mouth and finger as he worked me.

I'd been so worked up to begin with that I was so close. My brain shut down.

I felt the firm flick of Kemp's tongue. I heard the wet pumping of his fingers. I breathed in the musky scent of Gus's cum on my thighs. My own arousal. I looked up and saw two men, their gazes squarely on my pussy and their friend's head as he pushed me over the edge.

My muscles tensed, heat spread and sizzled through my body. I cried out, gave over, sunk into the most brilliant, blinding pleasure ever. I fought against their secure hold, but they wouldn't give. I was caught in the pleasure they could give me. No escape. Nothing but… bliss.

And that had only been Kemp's mouth. His fingers. I had three dicks to experience. As I caught my breath, Kemp lifted his head to kiss my knee and wipe his mouth with the back of his hand.

Oh, he was very pleased with himself.

And he should be.

Kemp pushed to his feet and began to strip.

Poe's hand slid down, ran over my pussy. I gasped and tore my gaze from the inches of gorgeous body Kemp was revealing to look at Poe.

"These curls, sweetheart, gotta go. Later, I'll shave you bare. For now, up."

He and Gus moved me about as if I were tiny, lifting me and maneuvering me so I was kneeling on the bed. They quickly rid me of my shirt and bra so I was bare.

Then they stopped. And stared.

Kemp, now naked and stroking his dick, stared.

"Holy shit," Poe murmured.

"She's gorgeous, isn't she?" Gus

asked. He cupped a breast. "They're fuller than I remember."

Poe's big hand worked the other. I felt the rasp of callouses against my tender skin.

"I'm... I'm big everywhere," I murmured.

My nipples had always been very sensitive and they were learning that now.

Their hands began to rove over my breasts, shoulders, waist, hips, ass and even over my pussy.

"You are big," Poe said, his hand squeezing my ass. "Just right for a guy like me."

"Get on all fours, baby girl," Kemp said, stepping up to the edge of the bed.

I knew as soon as I leaned forward and put my hands on the mattress, I'd be right in line to suck him.

I licked my lips.

Poe grabbed the box beside me on

the bed, ripped it open and pulled out a long strip of condoms.

"Suck Kemp's cock like a good girl and I'll fuck your pussy," Poe said as he shucked his clothes.

Kemp arched a pale brow as he continued to stroke himself. While Poe gave the command, I could say no. Right here, right now, I could yank my consent. Kemp was waiting, making sure I was choosing to obey.

Like he'd said, their dominance only worked if I gave them my submission.

I wanted them to have it. I was still buzzing from the orgasm, but my pussy ached to be filled. I'd been soothed, but not sated. I wanted more. I *needed* more.

I leaned forward, set one palm on the bed, then the other. I knew my breasts hung down, swayed. My ass stuck out and as Poe grabbed a condom and crawled onto the bed behind me, he could see everything. I wasn't just stripping off my clothes; I was bare to them in all ways. Emotionally, too, for they were taking me places I'd never been but always wanted to go.

Dark places. Naughty places.

Kemp's cock was bigger than Gus's. Thicker. While Gus's was darker colored, Kemp's was pale, like him. The crown was flared wide, pre-cum slipping from the slit in a steady stream. When he stepped close, I stuck out my tongue, licked it up. Tangy, salty flavor burst on my tongue.

His hips bucked and I opened my mouth to take the head in. It was warm against my tongue, hard, yet the skin was silky soft. Kemp stroked back my hair as I looked up at him. His jaw was clenched tight, but a smile formed on his lips. His pale eyes were heated and I knew I made quite the sight. His dick in my mouth as Poe opened a condom, the crinkly sound of the wrapper and the

134

sound of my slurping tongue the only sounds in the room. Except when I pulled in my cheeks and sucked, then Kemp growled. A burst of pre-cum coated my tongue and I swallowed it down.

Poe's hands settled on my hips, anchoring me in place as he pressed into me, only an inch or so. I clenched and squeezed, wanting more.

"I'm big, sweetheart. Ready to take all of me?" Poe asked.

I couldn't turn my head to look at him, my mouth full of Kemp.

"She'll take all of you, Poe," Kemp assured him. "She's only taking the tip now, but she can take more. Isn't that right, baby girl?"

I wiggled my hips as much as I could, eager for Poe to slide deep. Same with Kemp, I wanted him to fill my mouth.

"Don't worry," Gus said. "With three

men, you'll get more than just the tip." I felt a finger tap at my back entrance. Gus's finger. Oh god. Nerve endings that had yet to be awakened flared to life. I moaned around Kemp's dick. "In every hole."

As Poe slid deep, filling me with every huge inch and Poe cupping my nape and feeding me all those thick inches of meat, Gus's finger circled and pressed against my ass.

I wasn't used to so many hands, so many dicks, it was overwhelming. The feelings and sensations with three men's attentions focused on me was incredible.

Poe bottomed out, his thighs pressing against mine. I felt so full. And then he began to move, sliding out so I was almost empty, as if it was only my pussy lips clinging to him that kept him inside, then he thrust hard.

I moaned again and Kemp began to

fuck my mouth, carefully going deeper and deeper each time. I kept my eyes on him and he was watching me carefully, seeing how far he could go. I couldn't move my head to work him. Instead, he fucked my mouth as Poe fucked my pussy. Each deep penetration had Poe's balls slapping my sensitive clit.

"She's going to come. Aren't you?" Kemp asked, his hips moving a little faster. He barely touched the back of my throat. For someone on the brink of coming himself, he had tight rein on his motions.

"Her pussy's clenching so hard on my dick," Poe said on a growl.

Gus's finger breached my ass; the slight burn of it combined with the dark bliss of pleasure pushed me over the edge.

I came, my body jerking but not moving in their tight hold. I cried out, but my mouth was full of dick. My nipples pebbled to hard points, my skin bloomed with sweat. My pussy and ass clenched down, hard, in carnal ripples, wanting Poe deeper, to remain as far in me as possible. For Gus to slide his finger in even farther, to make everything so tight.

Kemp's fingers tightened on my neck as he pressed deep and groaned. His dick swelled and he pulled back. "Open."

I did as he commanded, even as the pleasure still coursed through me. He painted my tongue with his cum, his eyes glued to how he was filling my mouth.

Poe's loud slaps of flesh on flesh came right before I felt his fingers tighten on my hips. He roared as he held himself deep. I couldn't feel his cum coating me, for the condom did its job. While it was a thoughtful precaution, I ached to have him mark me, to coat me with his cum, to feel it slipping out of me, knowing there was too much of it to fit, especially the way his dick crammed me so full.

I whimpered when Gus slipped his finger from my ass.

Kemp's hand slid around and cupped my chin. I looked up at him and Gus. "Swallow."

I followed Kemp's command and closed my mouth, took his big load into my belly while his flavor lingered on my tongue.

Gus stripped in record time as Poe pulled out, dropped himself on the bed beside me, his big size making the bed dip. "Toss me a condom, Poe."

I sat back on my heels. My pussy was swollen and a little sore, but I knew I wasn't done. I didn't want to be.

Poe's hand slid down my back and he turned my head to kiss me. He was gentle, his tongue almost playful in comparison to Kemp's rough kiss from earlier. "So sweet," he murmured, tucking my sweaty hair behind my ear.

"Come to me, pixie. Take my dick for a ride," Gus said.

I pulled back from Poe's kiss, met his blue eyes for a moment. He nodded, then helped me move so I was straddling Gus's waist, his condom-covered dick sticking straight up in the air. He'd just come and yet was ready again.

He grinned up at me.

That was the guy I remembered, the one I'd fallen in love with all those years ago. The beard, of course, made him look older, but it seemed as if no time had passed.

Oh, I'd put on some weight. My boobs had gotten bigger and my hips wider. I had some wrinkles and definitely some cellulite. But they'd said nothing, hadn't mentioned any of my flaws. It was as if they didn't see any of them.

Gus was more ripped than I remembered. A smattering of dark hair on his chest was new. He'd been bare before, only a thin line running from his navel down to the thatch at the base of his dick. He had muscles now, a six-pack of abs that indicated he worked out, and often.

Eager, I lifted up on my knees and hovered over him, then lowered myself down, took him deep.

"Oh fuck, pixie," he murmured when I was sitting once again upon his thighs, this time with him buried inside me.

I couldn't remain still, so I moved, lifted and lowered, circled and rocked.

"That pussy's heaven, isn't it, Gus?" Poe asked. He was on his way back from the bathroom after disposing of the condom. I stopped moving and stared.

Poe was naked, and I finally got a glimpse of every inch of him. So big. Thickly muscled, dark hair on his arms and legs, a smattering on his chest. His cock pointed right at me, rock hard.

"This is our second chance, Parker," Gus said, and I looked back at him.

My hair slid over my shoulders and brushed the top of my breasts.

"I think Kemp may be right," I said, smiling at him.

He arched a dark brow. "Oh?"

"I think your dick *is* the smallest."

He gripped my hips then, held me in place. "Kemp, go get that plug you bought at the store. Our girl is a little too sassy for her own good."

My mouth opened, but he hooked a hand behind my neck and pulled me down for a kiss. His dick might be buried to the hilt in my pussy, but this was our first kiss in ten years. I remembered his lips, his taste, but the beard was new. I circled my hips as we kissed and kissed, my breasts mashed against his chest.

It was only when I felt a cold drizzle of liquid between my parted bottom cheeks did I lift my head. I looked over my shoulder. Kemp held up a butt plug. Turquoise and silicone. "Ever had something in your ass, baby girl?" he asked.

"Yes," I replied as his finger worked the lube over my crinkled hole. Instinctively, I tried to keep him out.

Poe, who'd been standing next to Kemp and watching, spanked me. "Let him in."

Of course, that only made me clench more and Gus hissed. "I'm dying here. I need to fuck her."

Kemp dropped the plug and grabbed a different one from the bedside table. This wasn't a plug, but a toy. A long line of silicone with little beads placed every inch or so, getting progressively larger until the end where there was a ring. A pull ring to hook a finger in to tug the beads out.

I clenched again.

"Fuck." Gus gripped my hips and fucked me, lifting and lowering me as he thrust up. He wasn't gentle and my breasts bounced. After, god, I had no idea how long, he stopped and I could catch my breath. I was close to coming, my clit rubbing against him as I moved, but it hadn't been *quite* enough.

"Now deal with her sass," he said, voice ragged, sweat dotting his brow. His face was flushed and he looked like a god. One with a big dick and also the one I'd teased.

And now more lube was being drizzled over my back entrance and worked in, followed by the beads. After the first one went in, I gasped. Gus pulled me down for a kiss and I knew this position gave Kemp a better angle to work my bottom.

I'd felt full with Gus's dick in me, but now, the beads, as Kemp pushed the next one carefully in, stretched me. More and then more still until another one silently popped within. The beads, along with Gus, made me feel so full.

Gus kissed away my whimpers, my moans as I took each and every one of those beads. I could only imagine what Kemp and Poe were seeing, how I'd not only swallowed up Gus's dick, but a row of silicone beads, too.

"Will we ever be able to curb your sass?" Poe asked, stroking back my hair.

"Doubtful," I replied.

Kemp gave a quick tug and one of the beads popped out. I gasped, arched my back and clenched.

"Oh my god," I moaned.

Gus grinned. "Maybe another orgasm will get you compliant."

He didn't say more, only moved me, fucked me, worked my body until I arched my back and came, the thick feel of his dick stroking over my g-spot—how did he do that?—set me off.

But it was when Kemp pulled out the beads, one right after the other that I screamed. The dual sensations of my clit and g-spot being rubbed and the anal beads offering dark and slightly painful pleasure, destroyed me.

I was a quivering, sweaty mess when Gus called out my name and came.

Someone helped me off of Gus, and I curled up on the bed.

"You're not done, Parker. Bad girls who sass get their asses fucked."

I was maneuvered once again, this time so I was leaning over the side of the bed. My feet were on the floor and a pillow was stuffed between my hips. More cool lube, this time though, it felt good on my worked tissues, followed by another condom wrapper opening.

A hand tugged one of my butt cheeks to the side, and a finger slipped into my back entrance. Nice and deep it went, working more and more lube inside.

"Isn't that right?" Kemp asked.

God, he was the dirty talker. The dark one. Poe might be intense and Gus laid back, but Kemp had a kink that matched my own. He was the one who'd push me, to give me what I didn't even really know I needed. Yet he was waiting for me to tell him yes.

I nodded into the pillow as a second finger joined the first, stretching me open wider than the beads had.

"I need the words."

"Yes, sir."

"Oh, so sweet. But yes, sir, what?"

I breathed in and out as he added a third. I'd done butt stuff before. This wasn't new to me, but it had never felt like this before. It had always been a guy wanting to ass fuck. Nothing more.

But Kemp was making me submit in the most intimate way possible. Making me admit I wanted it, making it seem naughty when it was anything but, especially between the four of us. But me, being a bad girl, only added another level of their domination.

"Yes, sir, I... I need my ass fucked."

Poe crawled onto the bed, knelt and parted his knees wide right in front of my face. His dick was right there. I smelled soap, as if when he'd gone in to dispose of the condom, he'd washed up in the bathroom.

"That's right," Kemp replied.

I whimpered and looked over my shoulder. Kemp's condom-covered dick —glistening with extra lube—was settled right between my cheeks, the head nudging the well-slicked entrance.

He prodded, pushed. Gus squirted more lube onto my entrance. Poe turned my head, focused my attention on him. "Suck my dick, sweetheart."

I gasped when Kemp popped past my tight ring of muscle. I was stretched open, so unbelievably wide, but it felt strangely good. Jangly. Intense. Dark. After I caught my breath, I took Poe into my mouth. He was slow, careful as he mouth fucked me. I glanced up, saw him watching his big slab of meat disappear in my mouth, but he would look down my back, watch as Kemp worked himself into me deeper and deeper until he bottomed out.

Only then did they move. Slow and steady. I felt... skewered. Dominated. Controlled. I couldn't wiggle, couldn't do anything except let them fuck me. Knowing that pushed me to the brink of coming. I'd never felt so submissive. Ever. When a hand worked its way between my hips and the pillow and found my clit, I came. Instantly. I dripped all over Gus's hand as I clenched around Kemp's dick, my pussy empty. Poe pressed his dick to the back of my mouth, the broad head sitting right at the back of my throat and he came. I swallowed his cum, down and down again before he pulled out.

Kemp continued to slowly fuck me until he, too, came. Deep in my ass.

I was done. Finished. Ruined.

"This is just the beginning, pixie," Gus murmured as he kissed my head, tucked me beneath the covers. "I'm not letting you go again."

"*We* aren't letting you go," Kemp added.

I must have fallen asleep, for the next time I opened my eyes, the room was dark and Gus's head was between my thighs. We were alone, the big bed just for us.

And hours later, as dawn turned the sky pink, I woke to Poe picking me up and carrying me—carrying!—to the bathroom and helping me into a hot shower. There, he settled me on the bench, parted my thighs and shaved me, just as he'd promised to do.

After, he fucked me, then left me a boneless heap.

If Kemp hadn't already left to go to the gym, I'd have been late for work. Even without a different kind of morning workout with him, I was deliciously sore and had a smile on my face when I walked to my sheriff SUV, Honey right on my heels.

9

KEMP

"*I* think Gus getting a second chance with Parker is really romantic," Julia said. She was setting out plates on the teak table, circling it and putting one in front of each chair. Her red hair caught the early evening sun and made it even more vivid.

For the Duke family weekly dinner, it was at the ranch since it was Tucker's turn to host. Even with Mr. and Mrs.

Duke not back yet from a Mediterranean cruise, the rest still got together. The weather was so nice we were eating outside on the large patio. The huge grill was hot and smoking, the scent of barbecued meat made my stomach growl. I was hungry, and not just for food.

Parker was to show up after her shift and I was eager to see her. My dick, too.

It had been hard to let her go this morning, content to keep her naked all day. Fuck, what we'd done with her. She'd been so responsive. It had been practically vanilla, what we'd done. We hadn't tied her up—or made use of her handcuffs—or spanked her... barely. She hadn't stayed naked all day so we could bend her over any available surface and fuck her. We hadn't put a plug in her ass and made her wear it. Hell, it wasn't like she could keep it in when she went to work, but I would certainly insert one and send her off to the market. Or get her on her knees after she came in the door, taking turns to suck all three of us off. My dick got hard thinking of my cum on her tongue, then her swallowing it down as if it were her favorite treat.

Yeah, I was ruined. Good thing, she was off the next two days, so every dirty kind of play was still a possibility.

But Julia's words made me smile and glance at Gus.

He was stroking his beard with his thumb and I had no doubt he was thinking what we'd done with Parker was anything *but* romantic. It had been filthy, at best. My mouth watered for the taste of her pussy again. Just remembering the way her inner walls had clenched my fingers when she came for me that first time or later, when I'd been balls deep in her tight ass. My dick wanted in her again.

"I'm not claiming her alone, you know," Gus told her.

She set the last plate down, then faced us. Smiled, although a little wistfully. "I know. I'm glad you guys found someone together. You've been waiting for a while."

As far as I knew, Julia wasn't dating anyone. She'd gone out with a few guys —Gus had grumbled about the simple dinner-and-a-movie dates she went on —but none stuck. None worth bringing to a Sunday dinner. No doubt she wanted to find The One herself, especially since all three of her brothers had. I smiled, realizing that was true. Gus had found his woman and she was mine and Poe's, too. Just yesterday we'd met her for the first time and yet, she was ours. For good.

I wanted to hug Julia, tell her the

VANESSA VALE

right guy was worth waiting for, that the right one would treat her like a queen or her brothers, along with Jed, Colton, Poe and I, would beat the fucking shit out of him. She knew it, probably felt the pressure of that alone, because any guy who wanted her would have to be so pussy whipped that he didn't care what all of us would do to him. Because if he so much as even had a dirty thought about Julia, let alone touched her, he'd have his hand lopped off at the wrist. And if he even considered doing half of the dirty stuff we did with Parker... he'd be buried somewhere on the ranch, never to be seen again.

But I didn't want to embarrass her, to make it obvious to her brothers she wanted her own romance, so I did nothing.

Julia went back inside. It was just the guys on the patio now. The women were in the kitchen. They'd left the grilling to the men, although I had no doubt they could do a perfectly fine job on their own. Gus, Colton and Jed were relaxing in Adirondack chairs while Tucker and Duke manned the grill—not that it was a two-man job. Poe was leaning against the railing.

"I'm surprised you're even here," Tucker said, lifting the lid on the grill and flipping a sizzling steak. While his nickname was T-Bone, he wasn't called that because of the beef his ranch produced. Hell, no. I had no doubt the well-satisfied look on Ava's face meant his dick was a serious piece of meat. And Colton wouldn't leave her wanting either.

"Did she sneak out at dawn because you didn't satisfy her? I'd think with the three of you giving it to her she'd get a *little* pleasure," Duke ribbed, holding his fingers close together.

"Yeah, little brother. If you can't figure out where her clit is, there are videos online," Tucker added with a grin.

Gus just stared at his brothers, clearly having learned not to give them any more fodder to fuck with.

"You get Parker Drew between you and you let her go off to work," Jed added. "Can she even walk right after taking on three dicks?"

Gus grinned and Poe frowned.

"I'm not even going to talk about how Parker takes us. You Duke boys can fuck around and joke," Poe grumbled. "But her heading off this morning to be the fucking county sheriff? Not my first choice." He went to the cooler and grabbed a can of soda.

"I thought Parker'd be the one to have something shoved up her ass, but you, Poe?" Tucker asked. They might kid and poke fun at our sex lives, but it was only brotherly ribbing. None of the guys would ever disrespect a woman for her sexual desires. And while Parker'd had my dick deep in her ass the night before, the three of us wouldn't have shared that with anyone. He was only poking fun at Poe. The jokes were always about the guy's performance, not that of the woman. She was able to fuck with wild abandon as much as any guy.

Poe stood, gave Tucker the finger, then popped the top on his drink. "You're protective of Ava. Would you let her take on Parker's job?"

Tucker's smile slipped and he was thoughtful for a moment, even glanced at Colton. Then he looked to Poe and nodded. "Point taken."

"She's ours, no question," Gus began. He was sitting in one of the Adirondack chairs with a glass of iced tea.

I knew Tucker and Colton saw Ava

once and knew she'd be theirs. Duke and Jed got a glimpse of Kaitlyn across the bar and were done for. So us seeing Parker for the first time yesterday, fucking her thoroughly last night and saying she was ours today was not out of the ordinary.

"But she's got a job," Gus continued. "An important one. Responsibilities. You didn't keep Ava from running the Seed and Feed after she finally said yes to being with the two of you."

"And Kaitlyn still works at the library," I added. "Speaking of not being able to walk right, you let her up for air sometime."

While I didn't think Duke and Jed were into having Kaitlyn submit, they were dominant men, and I had no doubt they took charge in the bedroom. But definitely not to the same extent as what Parker needed.

Jed grinned. "But she quit the job at

the hotel. At first, she hadn't been thrilled to have us help her financially, but getting her house fixed up and rented made her feel like she could hold her own. That she could be self-sufficient again."

"Not that she'll ever have need to be," Duke added.

I could see why Kaitlyn didn't want to rely on a man financially, especially since her dad had been a drunk deadbeat... and worse from what Gus had said. But I knew Duke and Jed. She was theirs and they had zero plans to let her go. Ever.

"And Parker's the sheriff," Tucker said, closing the lid. Smoke came out of the little vent at the top. "No way will she let you guys run roughshod over her. Hell, she'll probably Taser you if you even tried."

"If it kept her name off the ballot and had her handing that badge over to

Hogan or Beirstad, I'd let her Tase me," Poe said. The guys eyed him, but said nothing, obviously recognizing how serious he was about having her stepping down and letting someone else have her job.

The mention of Beirstad had Duke and Jed looking grim, but it wasn't Roger, the one who'd been fucking with Kaitlyn who was running for sheriff, but his older brother, Mark.

I didn't want Parker to be sheriff. It wasn't because I thought her underqualified or not good at her job. But shit happened. It made me nervous with the possible dangers she faced.

Poe wasn't alone in that thinking. But Parker wasn't the kind of woman to rely on a man. She might give over her control to us in the bedroom—or even the shower—but she kept it elsewhere. There was no fucking way she'd let us run roughshod over her as Tucker said.

If she wanted to add her name to the ballot for sheriff, we were going to have to support her in it. I glanced at Poe because I wasn't sure how he would handle that.

"She's smart. To be a lawyer, *really* fucking smart," Poe added. "There are plenty of other jobs out there for her. Jobs that don't require carrying a gun for safety."

"She could talk to Porter," Duke offered. "He's the DA and based in Clayton."

Poe frowned and I looked to Duke. "Is that your cousin?" I wondered.

"He's two years older than me. Grew up with us. His mom and our mom are sisters."

"Don't fuck with her, Poe," Gus warned. "She's worked hard for this job. For what she's built for herself. If this is what she wants, all of us have to respect that." He eyed the others as well before turning his attention to Poe. "Would you want her telling you to stop being a vet because working with horses might get you kicked?"

"When a horse carries a gun, then we'll talk," Poe countered.

Our attention turned to the sound of a vehicle pulling up, parking beside the others. Parker's sheriff SUV.

"Is that a dog in the front seat?" Duke asked, hands on hips. "I didn't know they had K-9 now."

"They don't." I grinned at Parker's new sidekick. She may not want a dog, or consider herself a dog person, but she had one now. Honey was in the passenger seat, sitting there as if she were Parker's partner. Ears perked up, her tongue hanging out.

"That's Honey," Gus said.

"That's what you call her?" Jed asked. "I call Kaitlyn sugar."

"The dog, you fucker," I said, going

past him. "But she does taste like honey." I went down the walk and over to Parker. Poe beat me to her, opening the door before she could do it herself. As soon as she climbed out, Honey followed then trotted off to explore and Poe pulled Parker into his arms and kissed her. It was a blatant kiss of a guy who wanted a woman. But there was an obvious hint of desperation to it, as if he held her to reassure himself that she was alive.

10

PARKER

"Spill, woman," Julia said when I joined the ladies in the kitchen. The scent of grilling meat followed me indoors. Spread out on the granite counter were plates with rolls, bottles of condiments, a basket of chips and a crock pot that had something bubbling inside. By the smell, I guessed baked beans.

I glanced between the three of them.

Julia Duke had gorgeous red hair—
where it came from, I had no idea since
she looked nothing like any of her
brothers—and a quick grin. Kaitlyn
pushed her glasses up her nose and had
a soft smile, as if she had a secret. Ava
looked all glamorous with her blonde
hair in beautiful curls down her back,
her nails a bright fire engine red.

I was off for two days barring any
acts of God and wanted to kick back
and enjoy the dinner. I hadn't seen
Gus's brothers and sister since high
school and had never met the others.
First impressions were important and I
figured a t-shirt and jeans were better
than a uniform.

But, my stick straight hair was
pulled back in a rubber band I'd found
on my desk and I wore zero makeup.
Looking at Ava, I felt ridiculously
unladylike. And that wasn't taking into
account I had several inches on them

and maybe forty pounds. I was ready for the roller derby while they were ready for a day at the mall.

I'd taken off my utility belt and put my service piece in the lockbox in the SUV. I'd even—much to Poe's, Kemp's and Gus's enjoyment—taken off my uniform shirt. They'd looked like horndogs by the side of the SUV as I undid the buttons, but sad little boys when a racy bra and bare skin wasn't exposed, but a plain white t-shirt.

"Spill what, exactly?" I asked.

"I thought Poe was a vet. I didn't realize he did tonsil checkups on people," Kaitlyn replied, waggling her eyebrows. "With his tongue."

I blushed. I could feel it. No one had missed the way he'd practically swallowed me whole. God, he was the intense one of the three. That fact that this morning he'd shaved my pussy bare with a focused diligence, then fucked me in the shower was a good example. He was also broody and wary. Needy in a way I didn't quite understand yet, but was almost tangible about him. It was as if he were frantic for me. Oh, Gus and Kemp were frantic as well, their dicks hard and eager to get inside me. But there was something else with Poe. I just didn't understand it yet. But that was okay. I liked it…whatever *it* was.

He smelled so good, and I remembered how I breathed in his clean scent along with the pungent scent of fucking. Of my juices, his cum, even though he'd filled a condom with it instead of my pussy.

I squeezed my thighs together, felt how sleek I felt being bare down there. I was wet, too. Still.

"I've got two men to handle. How you take on three…" Ava said, going to the fridge and pulling out a jar of pickles and handing them to Julia.

I shrugged. "I, um… don't really know the difference. It's not like I've ever done it before. They're a handful though."

Julia put her hands over her ears. "A handful? I don't want to hear that kind of talk about my brother!"

I stared at her wide-eyed, confused for a second, then Kaitlyn, Ava and I laughed. Ava grabbed one of Julia's hands and tugged it down. "She wasn't talking about the size of Gus's dick." She offered me a sly look. "But I'm sure it's much more than a handful."

Julia groaned.

"She was talking about dealing with three men," Kaitlyn clarified. "They're stubborn. Bossy."

"Opinionated," Ava added.

"Alpha," Kaitlyn replied.

"Dominant," I offered.

They stared at me and Ava grinned. She came over, patted my arm.

"Dominant, bossy alphas times three. Nice job."

"You talk as if Tucker and Colton don't tie you up and have their way with you," Julia said, opening the pickle jar lid.

Ava put her hand to her chest. "Me? What about little Miss Perv over here. She got it on with Duke and Jed *on stage* at a male revue show. And she didn't even know their names."

My mouth fell open. Kaitlyn, the librarian? Not only at a revue show, but *on stage?* Then I thought of Duke and Jed outside in their jeans and snap shirts. They knew how to fill them out all right. I didn't blame her. Hell, I'd bent over and showed my ass to three men in a vet clinic.

"So it's not weird that I saw Gus again after all this time yesterday, and I'd never even met Poe or Kemp before that? I mean, they're talking long term here and it's been…" I glanced down at my watch. "Thirty hours."

"Welcome to the club of men who know what they want—"

"More like *who* they want," Kaitlyn clarified.

"—and going after it. Getting it. And never letting go."

The way Ava talked, it was as if the same thing happened to her. When she held up her left hand and flashed a big diamond engagement ring, I had my answer.

Had Tucker and Jed been so intent, so serious so fast? The way Kaitlyn was nodding, and what Ava had said about how they'd done sexy times without even knowing each other's names… Duke and Jed were the same way.

"Is this a Duke thing? Lust at first sight? I mean, it's fast. You saw Poe and the tonsillectomy. I met him yesterday.

And the stuff we did last night… and this morning…"

I blushed and the women grinned. Ava even high-fived me.

Gus had said he'd always loved me. That made a little sense since we'd dated, known each other before we had sex. But Kemp and Poe? Ten minutes with them and I'd had my jeans pushed down over my thighs and thick stripes of Gus's cum across my butt. Another six hours and they'd been deep inside me.

We looked to Julia, who held up her hands. "Hey, don't look at me. I don't even have one guy, let alone two. Or *three*."

"It's definitely a Duke thing," Kaitlyn said. "And don't be hard on yourself. You deserve to take what you want. If that's three big dicks, then go for it."

"Kaitlyn!" Julia groaned.

"She's right," Ava added, ignoring

Julia. "Guys are allowed to fuck who they want, when they want. A quickie with a stranger in a bar bathroom. But women? Total double standard. I do know that Gus, Kemp and Poe wouldn't go after you like they are if they weren't in for the long haul."

"The Duke boys are one-woman men," Kaitlyn shared.

They made me feel a little better. A little less like a hussy. A hussy who had the best night of her life. With three men. With three really big dicks. And they knew exactly how to use them. And their hands. Oh, god, and their tongues. I was achy and a little sore from the way they'd taken me. Over and over and over.

"Well, regardless of the fact you're sleeping with my brother, I'm glad you're here," Julia said, breaking me from my pervy thoughts.

"I sleep with your other brother," Ava said.

"And I sleep with the other one," Kaitlyn added.

Julia rolled her eyes. "Fine. I get it. My brothers have sex lives and I have none. Let's talk about something else."

All three of them turned to face me.

I sighed. "What do you want to know?"

"Do you want a drink?" Ava asked.

"That's an easy one," I countered with a smile. "Water would be great."

"I remember you from high school. I was in tenth grade when you started dating Gus," Julia said.

I nodded. "I remember. You played the clarinet."

Horror crossed Julia's face. "I will pay you a million dollars to never mention that again."

I laughed as Ava handed me a glass

of ice water. "What? You played really well."

"Fine, if money won't work, I'll be your best friend."

"Oh, well, in that case then. I won't say anything about a musical instrument ever again."

Ava rolled her eyes and opened a package of hot dog buns.

"We've got enough, don't you think?" Kaitlyn asked, glancing at the ones already out.

With her free hand, Ava pointed out the wall of windows that overlooked the patio and took in the view of the ranch beyond. "There are seven men out there."

"Right. Never mind."

"You moved back to take the sheriff's job," Julia said. "That's pretty exciting."

My cell phone rang from my back pocket and I grabbed it as I answered her. "I moved back to be closer to my mom. She has diabetes now and I worried no one was helping her closely with it." I glanced at the screen. "Speaking of, it's her. Excuse me, I need to make sure she's okay." I swiped the screen, then put the phone to my ear. "Hi, Momma."

"Don't worry, I'm fine. Sugar's one-forty. It's something else and I wanted you to hear it from me first," she said.

"What?" I was relieved her sugar level was fine, but I dreaded what she would say next.

I heard her sigh.

"I got laid off."

What? "From the dentist's office? He can't possibly need to downsize."

I thought of Roger Beirstad. While he was a total asshat, he was one of the only dentists in town.

"He said I didn't fit in his practice any longer."

I frowned down at the hardwood floor. "Did he say why?"

"Actually, he told me to ask you. But that makes no sense. At least he didn't fire me."

She sounded dejected and I didn't blame her. She'd worked there for over a decade, being the office manager not only for Beirstad but for the old dentist who'd sold him the practice. While she couldn't clean teeth, she knew more about that office than anyone.

But what did I have to do with anything related to her job? I hadn't been in town long enough to need a cleaning. She'd started working at the practice right after I left for college. I'd been back to visit on breaks or long weekends, but nothing that might affect that.

"He can't just *fire* you," I countered. Well, he could. Montana was an at will state, meaning an employer didn't really need a reason to fire someone, but Raines was a small town. Word spread.

"Well, I'm glad at least I was given a small severance."

She told me the amount and I was pissed. For a decade of employment, she should have received at least twice that. But I didn't tell that to her. What good would it have done except upset her more?

"Momma, are you all right for now? I'm at the Duke ranch, but I can come over if you need me."

"The Duke ranch? Are you seeing Gus Duke again?"

"Something like that," I replied neutrally. Now wasn't the time to get into the complexities of that one, and there was no way I would tell her about last night. Or this morning in the shower.

"Oh, how nice. No, I'm fine. Really." Except she didn't have a job and she needed to pay for insulin and other diabetic supplies.

"Well, I'll check in with you when I'm done here."

"All right. I love you."

"I love you, too."

I ended the call and looked up. Kaitlyn, Ava and Julia were staring at me, obviously overhearing.

"Roger Beirstad laid off my mother. She was his office manager," I told them. As if Momma didn't have enough challenges, this was all she needed. I could support her, if need be, because I'd been doing quite a bit of saving, but neither of us wanted that. But jobs in a small town like Raines were few and far between.

"Why?" Ava asked, frowning.

I shrugged. "No longer a good fit, she said. Something to do with me."

11

PARKER

"*W*hat does that even mean? Ooh, I hate that guy," Kaitlyn said.

She told me about their one date, how he'd been demeaning and rude. How she'd turned him down but he'd made it a point to try and embarrass her in front of everyone at Cassidy's— Jed's bar downtown—one night.

Needless to say, the Duke family had shut that shit down pretty fast.

I hadn't heard about any of that, but Roger Beirstad hadn't done anything against the law so he hadn't come across my path.

Kaitlyn stomped to the back door and went out to Duke and Jed. We watched as Duke pulled her in for a hug.

"They're real careful with her," Julia commented. "She's had it rough. With her dad and all."

My confusion must have shown, for she added, "Her dad's the guy who hurt my parents in the hit and run."

My mouth dropped open. "Holy shit." I remembered the accident. Everyone in town over the age of twenty probably did.

"As for Roger Beirstad," Julia continued. "He's a total asshole and she gets bent out of shape because of him."

"They give her what she needs," Ava added. "Duke and Jed."

Kemp had told me he, Poe and Gus would give me what I needed, but this was something completely different. Kaitlyn needed comforting, not fucking. And the way Duke—as big as he was—held her so carefully, as if she were the most precious thing in the world, was amazing to see.

"I'm hiring," Ava said, breaking me from my thoughts.

I stared at her, wide-eyed. "What?"

"I'm living here pretty much all the time," she said. She waved her hand in the air indicating the ranch house. "Winter's coming and Tucker and Colton aren't excited about me driving on the roads in and out of town every day. It would be nice to have someone who lived close to the store to take on some shifts, to be available when I can't make it in."

"Wow, Ava," I replied. "I can't speak for my mom, but the offer sounds great. Maybe something different would be just what she needs."

"Have her call me at the store and we'll meet. If she's put up with Roger Beirstad, she can handle the Seed and Feed. Heck, she probably knows all my customers better than me—and their teeth."

Poe came inside, towered over Julia and Ava, but looked to me. His intensity was like a living thing, humming about him. "Is your mom okay? We heard what happened."

I shrugged. "I guess so. She's surprised and confused."

"And you?" His gaze raked over me as if I had been physically hurt.

I put my hands on my hips, sighed. "I'm pissed. She said I knew why she was laid off."

He frowned. "You know why she

was laid off or you were the reason for the lay off?"

I opened my mouth to answer, but took a moment to think. "Oh shit. You think Roger laid my mother off because of us? I met you for the first time *yesterday.*"

He shrugged his broad shoulders and remained silent.

I'd been mad for Momma, mad that Roger was such a total douche, but now, with what Poe was suggesting, it went deeper than that. Roger, who I didn't even know, hated me so much as to end my mother's employment.

"I'm not good for you," he said.

I glanced at him, then at Ava and Julia. I offered them a *what the fuck?* look. Julia stared at him wide-eyed and Ava just shrugged at me.

I blinked at him a few times before finally answering. "What?"

"Like you said, it's been a day, us

being together. Look what's happened. Imagine when the whole town finds out. And they will."

"Finds out, what? That I'm having sex with three men?" I all but shouted.

His eyes narrowed and his jaw clenched. "Excuse us, ladies," he said, taking my arm and leading me across the great room and into an office on the other side of the house. He closed the door behind me, offering us some privacy.

"You're not just having sex with three men, you're *in a relationship*," he clarified, crossing his arms over his big chest. "This is more than fucking and you know it."

I sighed, relieved. I did, but it was good to have Poe say it aloud. The kiss he'd given me when I arrived wasn't from someone who planned on fucking and forgetting. It had been as if he were memorizing me. But hearing it made me feel better.

Kemp and Gus came in the room, shut the door behind them, but not before Honey squeezed past and to my side. She sat down and leaned against me, setting her body between me and Poe, as if trying to protect me from him.

"What's going on?" Gus asked.

I reached down, pet the dog on the head, then crossed my arms over my chest. "Poe says he's not good for me. Yet he fucked me. So you what, wanted to get off before you got out of… this?" I waved my hand in the air, meaning all of us.

Poe narrowed his eyes at me. "That's sass and you should be spanked for it."

I put my hand to my chest. "*I* should be spanked?" Smoke was probably coming out of my ears. If Poe's goal was to redirect my anger at Roger Beirstad to him, he'd done the job.

"Don't make light of what's between us," he countered swiping his hand through the air. "Last night wasn't just fucking. It was our first time. Our *last* first time."

That was totally romantic and no doubt Julia would swoon over those words. But he hadn't been trying to do so, hadn't even realized he'd said something profound. But the vehemence behind it made Honey growl quietly.

I pet her again and she licked my hand. "Then what are you talking about?"

Kemp swore under his breath. Gus slapped Poe on the back. "Tell her, fucker, or I will."

Poe lifted his chin, shrugged off Gus's touch. "Fine. I said I wasn't good for you. I'm not. I murdered my father."

I hadn't expected that. Not at all.

Maybe he'd changed his mind about sharing me. Maybe he felt like his dick didn't measure up. Maybe he felt... oh, whatever. But not that.

"You murdered your father," I repeated. I'd heard him the first time, but my brain was slow to process. *Murdered?*

Poe nodded once. "I was sixteen. I went to juvie until I aged out at eighteen. My record's sealed since I was a minor, but still. The murderer and the sheriff. Not a good match, huh? I can ruin your career."

I laughed and rolled my eyes. "Like I've ruined my mother's?" I sighed. "This murder. Was it pre-meditated?"

He nodded again.

"Did he deserve it?"

His eyes widened as if he'd never been asked that before.

"Fuck, yes."

Kemp ran a hand over the back of his neck in frustration. "Jesus, Poe. You left out the fact that your dad would beat the shit out of your mom, out of you. For years. You killed him—not *murdered*—defending her."

No wonder he'd been so upset the day before when I told him about that domestic call I went on.

"Then why did you go to juvie?" I wondered. Sure, killing someone was a terrible crime, especially by a minor, but circumstances were always taken into account. I'd only known Poe for a day, but he wasn't a sociopath or deranged where he'd kill someone for no reason.

"They didn't see it as self-defense because my mom told the police she'd fallen down. Again."

"Your dad beat your mother, you killed him to get him to stop," Kemp elaborated. He sounded more frustrated by what happened to his friend than Poe did himself. "Then she protects her husband, the abuser, instead of her son, which makes the police put Poe away."

"I was this size at sixteen, maybe thirty pounds lighter. I didn't get this big from my dad."

"Holy shit," I whispered. I thought of Poe, a teenager, probably clumsy in his newfound size. Angry at watching his mother get hurt all the time. Pissed that he'd been beat up, too. Finally, he was able to do something about it, to protect her. And while he'd been a child —sixteen *was* a child in the eyes of the law—he was big. Bigger than most adults.

"She turned on you," I said softly.

The look on Poe's face was bleak. Angry. The tendons in his neck stood out. "Yes."

I closed the distance between us, wrapped my arms around him. Hugged him tight. I felt the beating of his heart against my ear, his ragged breathing. The tense lines of his muscles.

"Does anyone in town think less of you for what you did?" I asked. I couldn't see her, but I heard Honey circling us, her little nails clicking on the hardwood floor.

"No one knows outside of the Duke family. Kemp. Now you."

"Then it won't affect my job. And if it did, I'd tell them to fuck off."

"Will *you* think less of me? I mean, you're a lawyer. You stand for justice. And you're a cop."

I pulled back and looked up at him. "I do stand for justice. And it sounds like you handed it out."

"That's it?" he asked, surprised. His pale eyes were wide as if he were stunned it was just that simple.

"I told you, fucker," Kemp grumbled under his breath.

I felt Poe sigh, then he wrapped his arms around me.

"As for my mom's job, if it's because of us Roger laid her off, we'll deal with it."

"Yeah, but his brother wants *your* job," Gus said, moving to stand at my side. I looked up at him and he placed his hand gently on my shoulder. Now wasn't the time to tell him I wouldn't be sheriff after November. The damage to my mom—if it was because of Mark—was already done.

"So Roger fired my mother as what... retribution?"

Poe kissed the top of my head, breathed me in.

"Pettiness. Roger hates the Dukes," Gus said. "That's well-known to anyone in town. So if you're connected to us, then your mother's just collateral damage."

"See?" I replied. "It's not you who's bad for me. It's Gus since he's a Duke."

Poe loosened his hold, looked down at me. Smiled.

Finally.

"Like Honey," he reached out and gave her a pat. "I'm protective of what's mine, Parker. More so than any of the other guys. Can you handle that?" he asked.

"Yes."

"Good girl," he replied, and the praise felt good. "Have Gus or Kemp seen your bare pussy yet?"

My mouth fell open. That was quite a topic change.

"No."

"Show us, pixie," Gus said.

I looked around the room. A cross between an office and a library, a big desk in the center. I'd been to the house a bunch of times that one summer, but never in this room. No doubt it hadn't changed much since when it belonged to Mr. Duke—Gus's dad, specifically.

"Here?"

"Here," Kemp repeated, crossing his arms over his chest. "Now."

I swallowed, my heart racing. I loved the idea of doing something so illicit with a bunch of people just beyond a closed door. And I was the one getting naked—or at least halfway—in front of the men while they remained clothed.

Instantly, a calm settled over me. Quiet. They knew that exposing myself, showing them my pussy which Poe had thoroughly shaved, got me hot. My pussy belonged to them and they wanted to see it.

I was dripping with eagerness, for what would they do once I was bare? Slip their fingers in me? Fuck me? God, I wanted anything. *Everything.*

They stood before me, like three Titans, as I undid my jeans, worked them down over my hips, being sure to take my panties with them. Once settled about my thighs, my legs were pinned together and they couldn't see all that much.

Gus didn't seem to like that fact. "Turn around and bend over the desk."

"Good girl," Kemp added when I did so. "Ass out. Yes, like that. Now we can see your bare pussy."

"We did this yesterday, and again today," Gus said. "Maybe every day you should do this so you don't forget what's ours."

"She's not a good girl, she's a naughty girl," Poe added and I looked over my shoulder at him. "She's dripping wet. What have you been thinking about?"

"You," I replied.

"Just me?" he countered.

I shook my head. "All three of you."

"Fuck," Gus said, palming his dick while his eyes were laser focused on my pussy.

No, he couldn't.

"On your knees, baby girl. You've some cum to swallow."

Oh shit. It was so filthy, so... degrading, I loved it.

These weren't just any dicks, these were *my* dicks. And all three of them were hard and needy.

I knew the feeling.

I popped up and dropped to the floor, not bothering to fix my jeans. My bare butt rested against the heels of my boots.

All three of them opened their pants, but Gus stepped up first.

His hand tangled in my hair as I took him deep as best I could.

"Such a good girl. Take care of your men now... fuck," he growled as I sucked hard. "And we'll reward you all night long."

For now, dinner with the Duke family was forgotten. We were all hungry for something else. Me? I had three big dicks to swallow.

PARKER

*T*wo days off and I spent them naked. With three men, it had been easy for them to assure it. I'd pretty much gone from bed to bed to bed. Or couch to bed to shower to kitchen table. I'd been bent over, laid back, propped up and fucked so many different ways. They were inventive, dominant and wildly virile.

Butt plugs and handcuffs, rope and

even chocolate syrup had been brought in to play. They took me together, took me alone one at a time, and once just Poe and Kemp, with Gus having to pick up his parents at the airport. I'd submitted each and every time. To say they took control was an understatement, but I'd loved every minute of it.

I'd been out of my head, forgetting work, chores, everything. Heaven. *Orgasmic* heaven.

But time didn't stop for a new relationship. The men had animals to tend to. Vaccinations to give. Dogs to neuter.

I had a town to keep safe. I should have been relaxed with forty-eight hours off shift, but no. I needed coffee. Lots of it. I ached in muscles I didn't even know existed. I shouldn't even be walking right. Yet I had a smile on my face and a spring in my step as I walked from the station to the coffee shop a block away. I'd volunteered to do a caffeine run. Honey trotted along beside me, probably knowing she'd get a treat. While she didn't know where we were going, people knew she was my new sidekick and seemed to always have something for her. She was well-trained, but if it kept up, she'd be spoiled rotten and as fat as a barrel by Christmas.

The weather was holding for this time of year—there was just a hint of color to the leaves—and I had talked to Porter Duke to confirm the ADA job was mine after election day. I was excited about the prospect of getting back to litigating, but doing it in Raines instead of back east gave me a sense of… coming home.

I could be with Gus, Kemp and Poe, be close to my mom and have a dream job all at once.

"You!" someone shouted.

I turned to see the wife beater stomping toward me. He was cutting across Main Street and a car had to stop because of the jay walking. I hadn't seen him since we'd gone to his house for the domestic call a few days earlier. Then, he'd had a smug look on his face because his wife wouldn't press charges. She'd called 9-1-1 in the heat of the moment, but he'd somehow gotten her to change her mind.

But now, now he looked pissed. His dark hair looked greasy, his beard a few days past well-kempt, his jeans stained with what looked like grease and ketchup.

"You sent her away. Where the fuck is my wife?"

I stopped, set my hands on my utility belt. I'd been involved in altercations with belligerent people before, trained for them, but adrenaline still kicked in, my heart rate skyrocketing. At least I was right downtown and not out at his rundown house with no one around for at least a half mile.

"Sir, you need to calm down," I told him.

"Calm down?" He came up onto the sidewalk, got close. Too close. "My wife left me all because you showed up, told her that she didn't have to be slapped around. That bitch. I give her everything and then she leaves me."

His eyes were bloodshot and he smelled like a bar floor at last call on a busy Friday night.

"Sir, you need to step back, then walk away."

"Don't tell me what to do, you dyke bitch. How they made you a sheriff, a fucking woman, I have no idea. Tell me where my wife is or I'll—"

"You don't want to finish that

sentence. I'll ask you one last time. Step back, walk away and cool off."

His eyes flared wide and he raised his arm as if to punch me. Before I could react, Honey attacked, her teeth clamping down on the man's ankle. Deep growls came from her throat. I'd never seen her so aggressive, so vicious.

The man howled, kicked his leg as if to loosen Honey's clamped teeth. "Shit!" he shouted, reached down and punched Honey in the head.

I took his moment of distraction and the way he was bent toward the dog to push him further even more. With a sweep of his ankle—the one Honey had bitten—I took him face first to the ground.

People were out on the sidewalk now. I had one knee in the middle of his back as he swore and thrashed. I had his hands cuffed behind his back in seconds. I pulled my radio from my hip, but when I looked up, I saw two deputies running down the sidewalk. We were only a block from the station and someone must have called it in.

As he continued to cuss and belittle all women, I had a clear head to notice Honey. She was on her side, whimpering. Tongue hanging out. I couldn't move off of the fucker's back, but passersby knelt down and petted her.

I moved to let the deputies lift the guy to his feet.

"Take care of Honey. We've got him," one of them said as they gripped his upper arms and shoved him toward the station.

I dropped to my knees on the sidewalk right beside Honey. "Do you think she's okay?" I asked. I hadn't realized how much I cared for the dog until right then. She'd just been following me around, literally hanging out with me, until now. Now I realized she'd been watching out for me. I'd rescued her from the side of the road and she'd taken me on. And now, saved me in return.

A lump of tears lodged in my throat. I was more afraid something had happened to her than what that wife beater could have done to me.

The owners of the fishing and outdoor store we were in front of were checking her out. "We saw what he did," one said, his tone angry, but his hands gentle as he stroked and soothed Honey. "The fucker. Let's get her to the vet."

Right then, a woman went over to the car that was parked at the curb and hastily opened the back door. "My car's right here. Put her in the back seat," a woman said, waiting for the men to carefully lift Honey and put her in. "We'll get her to the vet."

POE

I come out of exam room two with Mrs. Mitchell and her cat to discover the small lobby in chaos. Well, not quite chaos, but there were at least six people and only one pet, a tiny dachshund sitting on a woman's lap. I was used to dogs barking, hissing from cats and even the constant squawking of a bird, but not so many people talking all at once. And at the center of it was Parker.

I said goodbye to Mrs. Mitchell and went over to her, got her attention by placing my hand on her shoulder.

She looked up at me and smiled. In her usual uniform shirt and jeans, her radio was turned low but it was noisy with communication. It had been only a few hours since she'd walked out of the house to go to work, not before she bent over the kitchen counter, pulled down her jeans and showed her men her pussy. Gus had been keeping that sweet treat shaved smooth.

She wasn't here to play, to continue where we left off that first day back in the kitchen. Something was up.

"What's going on?" I asked.

"Honey was protecting me from someone and the guy hit her."

Jesus. "Is she all right?" I didn't see her anywhere.

Parker pointed down the hallway. "She's in one of the rooms with Gus and Kemp, but they said she seemed fine after a quick look. They're taking x-rays to make sure."

I sighed, relieved. Honey was a great dog.

"What do you mean she was protecting you?"

"The guy from the domestic dispute the other day approached me on Main Street."

Holy fuck. That fucker went after her? I went instantly angry. My heartbeat was pounding in my ears and my fists clenched. If I had a little barometer, it would be close to exploding right now.

"Approached?" I asked.

"He was drunk and furious," Tom, from the sports store said.

Even worse. A drunk wife beater going after my girl.

His partner, Lucas, nodded in agreement. "As if the sheriff here would know where his wife went."

"Where's the guy now?" If he was out there, I was tracking him down. I'd killed one man; another wouldn't be a problem. Especially if he'd intended to hurt Parker.

"In custody. He'll be charged with assaulting an officer of the law and cruelty to animals."

"That's it?" I asked, wiping my mouth with the back of my hand.

Parker's eyes widened slightly, as if noticing I was about to turn into the Incredible Hulk.

"For now. That will hold him. If we can find his wife and get her to press charges for the injuries from the other day, we can pin more on him."

"For what he did today, he'll only get a fine. A warning," I assumed.

She shrugged. "Probably. Or serve thirty days if he has priors."

Thirty days.

"He'll come after you again." I sighed, looked at the ceiling trying to calm myself. "That's it, sweetheart.

You're quitting. I won't have you put in danger like that."

Her mouth fell open as she blushed hotly. "I did my job, Poe. I did it by the book."

"She did. Got that guy to the ground and he's huge. And drunk by the smell of him," a woman who'd been quiet until now said. Besides her, there was Marge, the florist and two other women I didn't know watching us. I had to guess they'd all seen what happened and had come with Parker to take care of Honey.

The woman's words didn't help at all. "Exactly. Big and drunk," I said. "You'll give notice to the city council and have Beirstad or Hogan cover until the election."

She crossed her arms over her chest. "And what will I do for a job?"

"I talked to Porter Duke at the DA's

office and you can work there. No weapons, no assholes coming after you. Safe." After the barbecue at the ranch, I'd gotten in touch with Porter, told him about Parker. Her qualifications. He'd been interested, but hadn't said much more as he'd had to go to court. It had eased my mind though, knowing my woman wouldn't be in danger every day.

"You got me a job because you think my decision to be sheriff is a bad one?"

"A dangerous one," I clarified. "Why put yourself at risk when you can be safe?"

She was all but vibrating with frustration. "Because it's what I want to do, Poe! You don't get to decide something like this."

I put my hands on my hips, stared her down. I could see out of the corner of my eye everyone else was watching us like a tennis match. Back and forth their heads turned.

I didn't give a shit about any of them. Only Parker. "Watch that sass, sweetheart, or you'll be over my knee getting your ass spanked faster than you took that fucker down."

Her mouth fell open and she stared at me. Wide-eyed. Blushing furiously.

The ladies laughed.

"I can't believe you just said that." As I watched, all fight left Parker. It was as if she... wilted before my eyes. For the first time since I met her, she looked weak. Were those tears in her eyes? She turned away, looked to Tom and Lucas. "Tell Gus to keep Honey."

She turned and left, not looking back. The waiting room was silent and everyone was staring at me. Why did I feel like she wasn't just walking out of the vet clinic, but out of my life?

13

GUS

"*W*hat the fuck did you do?" I asked Poe.

Mr. Monroe's corgi was the last patient of the day and the door was locked behind him. It was finally quiet. Honey was staring up at me, her head cocked to the side.

The x-rays hadn't shown any issues, which was what we'd assumed, but it was possible if the guy hit her just right, she could've cracked a tooth. We'd have to watch for an abscess, but she seemed fine. A little lonely without Parker. But who wasn't?

This was the first time we'd been able to corner Poe since earlier, the afternoon had been booked solid.

But now he spilled what he'd done— what he'd *said*—and I was ready to kill him.

Poe ran a hand over his dark hair, and winced when he finished. It was as if saying it aloud made him realize how much of a dumbass he was. "I fucked up."

"Really?" Kemp asked. He was a pretty even-keeled guy. Not much got to him, but this? Kemp was pissed. "You blew it with Parker. Jesus, Poe. She isn't your mom. She isn't that woman who got beat up by her husband. The one who thankfully got smart and left him."

He paced the lobby. "I know, but that guy went after her!"

"And she took him down," I added. Yeah, I wasn't too thrilled with the idea of a drunk asshole coming after our woman either.

"Fine, you were overprotective," Kemp offered. "She could understand that. Hell, she already forgave you for that, understood why when you told her about your dad. On top of that, no doubt Kaitlyn and Ava have shared how possessive their men are. I get that. *She* gets that. But you told her you'd spank her ass?"

"In front of Tom and Lucas?"

He swore under his breath. "And Mrs. Mitchell, Corrinne Borden and Marge."

"From the florist shop?" I asked. This was worse than I thought. I closed my eyes and took a deep breath. "She's the biggest busybody in the entire town! You used Parker's kink against her. Turned her submission into something shameful in front of others."

"I know, I know." Poe groaned. "I didn't mean it. I was just so angry that it just came out."

"And what's this about Porter? Didn't we tell you at the barbecue to lay off?"

He glanced at me with those weird pale eyes. He was pissed, too. Yeah, I'd just scolded him, but he fucking deserved it.

"I was trying to help. To find her a job where she wouldn't have to be in danger. Where I might be able to breathe."

It made sense. It did. But it didn't make it right.

"I want to keep her naked and tied to my bed, but that doesn't mean I'm going to do it," I countered. "She's a grown woman. She's got an advanced degree and police training. If you stifle her, she won't be the woman we all love."

Yeah, I loved her. I always had. This past week, fuck, had proved that sometimes people had a second chance. I just had to hope Parker would give Poe one.

"And fuck, Poe, spanking her ass? You just took a beautiful thing she gave us and turned it filthy."

Kemp looked at his phone. "She's not responding to texts." He glared at Poe. Pointed. "You're going to fix this. I don't care how you have to grovel. Beg. Plead. Hell, let her spank your ass in front of the entire town. Just fix it."

There was nothing else Kemp and I could do. We could track her down and tell her to reconsider how much of an idiot Poe was, but it wouldn't work. Poe had to apologize. Make this right. He had to get whatever fucking demons were driving his actions out of his system, and the only way to do that was bare it all to Parker. Again.

I went to the front door, flipped the lock.

"Where are you two going?" Poe asked.

I looked at my watch. "Town council meeting. Parker will be there. We'll make sure she's okay, that there's no fallout from what happened."

"Great, I'll come, too," he replied.

Kemp stopped Poe by a hand to his chest. "No fucking way. Come up with how you're going to fix this shit. *In private.*"

ARKER

· · ·

I didn't have time to sit at home and feel sorry for myself. I was so angry at Poe I wanted to track him down and Tase him, the dumbass. It wasn't as if he would miss any brain cells. Unfortunately, the monthly city council meeting got in the way of any that. As sheriff, I had to offer a report on calls since the last get-together and any other issues I might want to share. The council, in turn, brought things to my attention as needed. Last month, they let me know a four-way stop had been put in on the south side of town and to expect many people to blow through it.

The meeting was in the community room at the library and I waved to Kaitlyn as I went in. I didn't dare stop to chat at the check-out counter or she'd see I was upset and get me talking. The last thing I wanted to do was to cry before the meeting. It wasn't well-attended, perhaps ten to twenty people besides the council, depending on agenda.

It was my mother and Mrs. Duke chatting together inside the multi-purpose room which took me by surprise.

"Parker, sweetie, I thought I'd come and say hi," Momma said. "These days I never know where you might be."

I leaned in, kissed my mother's cheek, taking a moment to wonder if she meant I was busy, or that I'd spent more time at the men's house than my own. That I'd been in a haze of newfound lust—and love?—ever since I took Honey to the vet. And that thought made my heart lurch, my cheeks get hot. I'd forgotten about Poe's actions for all of a minute.

"I'm glad you're here," I replied.

Momma was fifty-five and I looked

just like her, although she was five-four and petite in figure. I got my size from my dad, although I'd only seen pictures of him because he'd died in a work accident three months before I was born. She always had a smile on her face and a nice thing to say about everyone. I always wondered why she hadn't remarried, but never pushed. She was involved in so many activities around town—a bowling league, teaching Sunday school and even learning French—that she seemed content.

"I talked with Ava Carter and I start at the Feed and Seed on Monday." She smiled almost brilliantly, clearly excited about her new job.

"That's great." It really was. An understanding boss was important now, especially if she had doctors' appointments or needed to rest for a bit because of her sugar levels.

"I know nothing about animal feed or machinery, but if I can learn about teeth and dentures, I can probably figure it out."

Mrs. Duke laughed, her chin length hair swaying. She was quite tan from her cruise. "Dottie, a new beginning for you. I don't speak ill of too many people, but I'd think not seeing Roger Beirstad every day will be a wonderful change."

Gus and I may have headed off to college and not talked for ten years, but Momma and Mrs. Duke had kept up and, while perhaps not close friends, liked each other very much.

Momma laughed. "You're right. I feel... liberated."

Mrs. Duke had always been so nice to me. Hell, she was nice to everyone. I remembered being the nervous girl who'd dated Gus and Mrs. Duke had always made me part of the family. Had me over for dinner and one time took me for a manicure with her and Julia. "Ava is a sweetheart and it will make Colton and Tucker feel better knowing she's not driving that stretch of road between the ranch and town when the snow begins to fall. You'll be an asset to all of them."

"It's nice how they're so protective," Momma added.

"All my boys are that way." Mrs. Duke turned to look at me, her graying brow arching up. "They take after their father. They mean well, but sometimes you want to strangle them. Gus was like that when he was younger, wasn't he, Parker?"

I nodded. Gus had been possessive and bossy even at eighteen. "Yes, ma'am."

"And now?" she asked pointedly.

I glanced at my mother, who eyed me with eagerness. They knew about

Gus, Poe and Kemp, but wanted confirmation. I wasn't sure if Gus told his mother we were together or if the small town grapevine had picked it up. Either way, I was in no place to deny it. Mrs. Duke's older two sons were in relationships where two men claimed one woman. It wasn't as if being with Gus, Poe and Kemp would be shocking to her now. And Momma didn't have her head in the sand. It might be a little weird for her to adjust having her daughter be with *three* guys, but I knew she only wanted me happy. One man or three, she probably was eager for grandkids, just like Mrs. Duke. I wasn't ready to give either of them any, but it was a step in the right direction.

"More so," I replied.

Both women beamed and Momma pulled me in for a squeeze. "Oh, sweetie, I'm so happy for you. Those three men are beyond handsome. And thoughtful. They went door to door last March when that big blizzard hit and made sure everyone had power and heat."

"They're bossy, too," Mrs. Duke added. "Be prepared to stand your ground."

The council members moved to their seats at the front of the room. Mrs. Duke patted me on the arm and said, "Glad you're finally part of the family again."

I stared after her as she walked away, then took a seat beside Momma as the meeting began.

I tuned it all out, replaying everything Poe had said. Even now, hours later, I felt my cheeks heat with embarrassment because the guys from the outdoor store knew that Poe spanked me, and not for fun. Well, not *just* fun. He'd made it seem I couldn't be self-sufficient, that I needed someone to control me because I was wild and perhaps dangerous to myself. He'd used my darkest desires against me, and that was what hurt. What shamed.

I'd given them… *him*, my trust, the most secretive part of me, and he'd belittled it all.

I liked that the three of them were possessive, that they *would* protect me. I felt a foot shorter and fifty pounds lighter, like a dainty female who had Neanderthals watching out for her when I was with them. I felt feminine in a world—and a job—that made me feel anything but. Poe had made his thoughts on my job well-known. He hated me being sheriff. While it *was* kind of him to talk to Porter Duke about a job, it had been done in poor taste.

Obviously, Porter hadn't said anything to Poe about me starting to work at the DA's office in November. It wasn't his place to share and I respected him for it. I could have told the guys at any time that I wasn't putting my name in for the sheriff's job, but we'd been pretty busy not talking.

Now I was glad I hadn't said anything, for Poe's true feelings had come out. I knew where I stood with him and it wasn't as an equal. It wasn't as the woman who gave my control over to them as a gift. He'd taken it and used it like a weapon against me.

"Sheriff Drew," one of the council members called. "Your update, please."

I stood, but didn't move to the front of the room. It was small enough where everyone could easily see and hear me from where I was. I'd prepared this morning for the meeting and read from my notes I'd pulled from my pocket. It only took a few minutes to cover my list and I sat back down.

Momma patted my arm, leaned in and whispered, "I'm so proud of you."

Because of her kind words, I almost missed someone say, "I'd like to speak to the council about the sheriff."

There were a few murmurs and Mark Beirstad stood. I took a deep breath, let it out. Momma took my hand, squeezed it. I flicked a glance her way and saw her jaw was clenched. She wasn't over what Mark's brother—her boss—did to her and she was smart enough to put the puzzle together. I was the missing piece.

Mark was in his early thirties, hair receding at a pace faster than he could grow a comb-over. His belly rolled over a large belt buckle, indicating he had won a few rodeo events in years past. He ran the local grain elevator and was very eager to be sheriff. He took moments like this often to share his feelings about something, or someone, in the community not to his liking. He liked to grandstand, even on a small scale. The fact that he had everyone's attention only made him roll his shoulders back and preen like a peacock. More like a cock.

"The sheriff is a civil servant, one who serves the community. He, *or she,* is a representative of the town."

Momma made a huffing sound at the blatant dig at putting my gender's pronoun as an add-on.

"Mark, we're all aware of the sheriff's role and that *she* serves the community," the mayor replied. He was in his fifties, easy to like and even easier to work with and because of this, was in his third term.

"Yes, but it has come to light that she's now involved with three men."

Beirstad stared pointedly at me. I lifted my chin and met his gaze head on.

I'd been shamed once by my choice today. I wouldn't be again.

"Cavorting in such a way is not an example we want set for our youth. I move to have her removed from office and replaced."

Murmuring broke out across the room and the mayor raised his hands. Everyone fell silent.

"Issues with county employees should be brought to human resources," the mayor added. "Not aired at a council meeting. Any breach of employment is considered by that staff. *Confidentially.*"

I had a gun. And a Taser. I could cross the room in a few steps and have Mark flailing on the ground peeing himself. I could stand up and say something, that what Mark said was true. I was in a relationship with three men. But I wasn't ashamed of it. I had no idea what I was going to do about

Poe, if I'd be able to remain involved with him. If who I was would be too much for him. But I *had* been with them. It was a fact and I couldn't change the past, nor did I want to.

"HR has no control over the election though," Mark countered. "I request a vote to have her name stricken from the ballot."

The council members looked back and forth at each other. The mayor remained silent, let Mark's words sit heavily. I glanced at Mrs. Duke. Oh, she didn't like Mark, that was for sure.

"Let me repeat for the record," the mayor began, looking to the secretary, who nodded. "Mark Beirstad has issues with Sheriff Drew's performance. He requests her name struck from the November ballot for the position."

"That is correct," Mark confirmed with a single nod.

"You are aware that it is one of Mrs.

Duke's sons who is in a relationship with the sheriff." Obviously, my love life was known by everyone. "Is there a reason, Mr. Beirstad, why you aren't complaining about the performance of Mrs. Duke as a council member? Not only is Gus Duke *cavorting* with the sheriff, but her other two sons are in similar kinds of relationships."

Mrs. Duke remained silent and stared down Mark.

He had the good grace to blush, but it was probably more out of anger than embarrassment.

"Also," the mayor continued. "The sheriff's mother is sitting right beside her. I would think that these two women would be quite vocal, perhaps more than you, if they had issue with the sheriff's actions."

No one said a word.

"The people of Raines can decide for themselves about the sheriff based on her performance on the job these past few months. That can't be said for you, Mark. They can and will, though, decide on you based on your comments here tonight."

Beirstad held up his hands. "Now, Mayor, this isn't about me. It's about the ballot on election day and having the right names on it."

"I wasn't aware, Mr. Beirstad," Mrs. Duke said. "That Sheriff Drew's name was on the ballot."

The mayor nodded. "Sheriff Drew, on her first day of work, made it clear she was just a fill-in and would not be seeking election."

"What?" Mark said, turning to look at me. His eyes looked like they belonged to a cartoon character, bugging out of his head. Obviously, this was something he hadn't known. "You aren't running for the job? Why didn't you say something?"

"Why should she have to?"

Everyone turned to the far side of the room as Liam Hogan—the previous sheriff's son—spoke. He stood, hat in hand, his hair neatly combed. He wore jeans and sturdy boots, a white button up shirt with the sleeves rolled back to show sturdy forearms. He helped run his family's small ranch and was a part-time deputy. His eyes were on me. Not anything like the way Gus, Kemp or Poe looked at me. There was no heat. Respect, perhaps, but it was purely professional.

Liam was two or three years older than me. I remembered him from growing up, but we hadn't been in the same friends' circles. I was sure he missed his dad; he'd been a good sheriff and it would be an honor for Liam to follow in his footsteps as sheriff. He had my vote, not because I didn't want Beirstad anywhere near a position of power... or a gun, but because he was the right man for the job.

"Leave Parker Drew alone, Mark," Liam continued. "Her personal life is just that, *personal*. She's more qualified for the role of sheriff than either of us. If Raines was lucky, she'd put her name in."

My cell vibrated and I glanced at the screen. Pam, the dispatcher, knew to send me a text if something was important, but not a true emergency. For that, my radio on my hip would beep.

*P*am: Poe was picked up. You should come to the station.

I read the short message twice. My heart skipped a beat. What had Poe done?

I stood then, my focus on the meeting completely shot and I had no time for Beirstad. "Thanks, Liam. It's nice to hear you say that. Your dad was a good role model to follow." I looked to the council at the front of the room. "Mr. Mayor, if I'm no longer needed, I'll let you finish your meeting and get back to work."

The mayor nodded and I peeked at Mrs. Duke. She looked a mix of furious and thoughtful. I had no doubt she wanted to say something to Mark, but was too much the lady to do so.

"You don't have anything to say for yourself? For your actions?" Mark asked me, shaking his head slightly as if scolding a toddler.

"All this meeting has done, Mark, is share *your* actions," I replied. I refused to stoop to his level, to get in a dialogue with him. That was what he wanted, but I had nothing to say. I had no *reason* to speak at all. "They speak louder than anything I could say."

I nodded to the council and turned. There, leaning against the back wall just inside the door were Kemp and Gus. Sitting between them was Honey. Her tongue was hanging out and she looked like she was smiling at me.

God, Gus and Kemp looked good. Big, brawny, even sexy. Cowboys through and through. I ached for them, wanted to walk up to them, have them pull me into their arms and never let go. I was used to dealing with little shits like Mark. But I didn't have to do it alone. I didn't *want* to. But there was something missing. *Someone.*

Poe.

And he was in my jail.

PARKER

$\mathcal{I}$ stopped once we were on the sidewalk in front of the library. The sun had just set and the air was cooler, and I felt a hint of fall. Momma had joined us and was leaning down and petting Honey behind her ear. The dog had her eyes closed as if she were in heaven.

"I finally meet the new dog. And the

new men," Momma said. "Well, Gus. You're not all that new, are you?"

Gus laughed. "Old *and* new. Good to see you again, Ms. Drew," he replied, taking her hand and leaning down to buss her cheek.

"This is Kemp," I said, settling a hand on his forearm. His skin was warm beneath my palm and the muscles there were corded, reminding me of how powerful and intense he was.

"Ma'am," he replied in his panty-melting deep voice, offering her a smile and a nod. Well, it melted *my* panties at least.

"You're missing one," Momma stated.

"Yes, we're going to go meet up with Poe now," I offered. I wasn't going to tell her he was in jail. While I *was* missing him, I wasn't sure if it would be a permanent thing or not.

"Why don't you join us for Sunday

dinner?" Gus asked. "It's a Duke family thing and my turn to host."

Momma smiled. "That would be great." She looked between the three of us. "I'll get the address from Parker."

"Let me walk you to your car," Kemp offered.

She held up her hand. "No need. It's right there." She pointed down the street and I saw her sedan only four cars away.

I gave her a hug and she walked off. Surprisingly, Honey followed. Mom stopped and looked down, then back at us. Honey looked up at her with adoration.

"She can go with you," I said. Honey glanced at me, then back at Momma and stayed at her side.

"She's your dog," she countered as she smiled down and pet Honey some more.

"I'm not so sure about that."

"I'll bring her to the station tomorrow."

Once she and Honey were in her car and driving off, Gus pulled me into his arms.

"Are you all right?"

I frowned with my cheek against his shoulder. He smelled good, he felt good. Sturdy. Dependable. "You mean about Poe?"

"That, too," Kemp said. "But about in there." He tipped his head toward the library.

"Beirstad doesn't bother me."

"Why didn't you say you weren't in the running for sheriff?" he asked.

I stepped back and shrugged. While I wanted to stay in Gus's arms, we were on the street. "It never came up. It hasn't been a week, Kemp. I mean, I know your parents are in Minnesota, but I don't even know if you have any brothers and sisters."

He nodded. "Point taken."

"And to be honest, you guys didn't ask."

"I think someone's missing out on this conversation. Let's go find Poe," Gus replied.

"He fucked up, baby girl," Kemp added. I had no doubt the three of them had talked after I left earlier.

I sighed, remembering Poe's words. *Watch that sass, sweetheart, or you'll be over my knee getting your ass spanked faster than you took that fucker down.*

They'd been said out of anger, out of emotion, although those words often offered the deepest insight. And that wasn't all of it. He'd gone behind my back and gotten me a job. A *safe* job. "Yeah, well, I think he might have fucked up again."

When they stared at me in confusion, I added, "He's in jail."

$\mathcal{P}$OE

$\mathcal{I}$ swore once I got out of juvie that I'd never be behind bars again. The claustrophobia of being locked away was something I would never forget, that still woke me up at night. But I did it for Parker. I had to get her to see me, to listen to how sorry I was. How much I fucked up everything.

I couldn't have her walking away. Stupid of me? Perhaps. Desperate? Definitely.

She was the best thing that had ever happened to me. Hands down. I didn't deserve her, obviously, since I was sitting once again behind bars. It hadn't even been a week, but I was done for. Everything we shared, in bed and out, had been the closest, deepest relationship I'd ever had. And sharing her with Kemp and Gus... fuck, it made us a family.

I wanted a family. Ached for it. And yet I'd blown it before we'd barely begun. My past, my hang-ups reared their ugly head and now she hated me. I had a feeling she'd forgive me for talking with Porter—she knew I was a protective bastard—but it was what I'd said that was so much worse.

I'd used her submission against her. I'd disrespected it. *Her.* Shamed her. Made what she gave to me, to the three of us, willingly and with blind trust, into an embarrassment.

It was a beautiful thing, her submission. It made me so fucking hard for her, but it made me love her, too. Deeply. Purely.

And I'd taken that trust and destroyed it.

I stood, paced the small cell. I felt like a caged animal, not because of the bars, but because of my feelings. I wanted to rip my skin off, to shout, rage with frustration. I just had to hope she was merciful and forgiving. That she'd give someone who was as fucked up as I was a second chance.

I didn't deserve it, but I wanted it. *Needed* it.

So I'd talked with Liam Hogan. We'd been friends for a while, involved in a monthly poker night. He'd told me where he was and I went flying past him in my truck going ninety in a fifty-five zone. He'd had no choice but to pull me over. I told him he had to put me in a cell. A ticket was all he'd offered, but I threatened him with breaking his nose so I'd get an assaulting an officer charge if that was what it took.

I'd explained I needed to get in front of Parker. Thankfully, he'd somehow understood I was pussy whipped—and in the dog house—with the sheriff. He was also smart enough to know I would do whatever it took with Parker and was content to keep his face arranged as it was, so he'd opened the back seat of his cruiser like a chauffeur and I climbed on in.

And finally, two hours later, Parker came in. Gus and Kemp followed, but leaned against the concrete wall and crossed their arms. They were going to listen, but I could tell they had no intention of getting involved. They were right, I had to fix this. It was on me.

She stood before the bars looking perfect. Sexy as hell. But her eyes didn't have that fierce, powerful woman gaze I was used to.

Wariness was there. Emptiness, too. All because of me.

"I'm sorry," I said.

Her dark brow winged up, but she said nothing. Her hands went to her utility belt, and she tucked her fingers in.

"I told you I was protective." I moved to stand right in front of her, my hands gripping the bars.

"Possessive. I warned you."

"You can't put the blame on me," she countered.

I sighed. "I'm still fucking things up. Sweetheart, but now you know how much. I shouldn't have gone to Porter Duke about a job. That was wrong. You're smart and capable without me. But I'm struggling to deal with the fact the woman I love might be hurt. Or worse."

Her mouth fell open and she just stared.

"Yes. Love. There are so many wives whose husbands are police or sheriffs or whatever and struggle with the possibility that they might not come home at the end of shift. Some deal, some don't. I'm trying. I *will* try."

She nodded, but didn't say anything.

I took a deep breath, let it out. "But the other. I'm sure I hurt you far worse. You gave me something precious and I... I... fuck."

Tears filled her eyes and I reached through the bars to brush one away. "Your submission is perfect. Beautiful. I should never, *never* have thrown it back in your face. If you'll give me a second chance, I promise, *vow,* to do everything in my power to gain your trust back."

"I'm taking a job with Porter Duke at the DA's office," she said.

She hadn't moved, let me stroke my thumb over the silky skin of her cheek.

"No. I won't let you. You're the sheriff and you shouldn't give that up because one of your men is a dumbass."

"You are a dumbass," she agreed. "But I'm not taking the job because of you. It's been arranged since summer. It was part of my contract that this was only temporary. Porter's been waiting for me to start after the election."

"But what about—"

"She never put her name on the ballot," Kemp said, stepping toward us.

I looked to him, then Parker. "You never—"

She shook her head.

"Why didn't you say?"

She shrugged. "It never came up."

Fuck, I wouldn't have turned into a fucking lunatic if I'd known, if her job had been temporary. "I'm glad it didn't," I admitted. "I made a shit show of

250

things because of it, but now you see who I am. And I know who you are. Independent. Strong. Brave. Fierce. I can't stifle any of that because that's what I love about you."

She leaned forward and we kissed, our foreheads pressed into the bars.

Ah, the sweet feel of her lips. The feel of my heart opening and letting Parker settle within.

She took the keys from her belt to unlock the cell door.

"Think twice about letting him out, pixie," Gus said. "You've got him completely at your mercy."

I smiled, but didn't tear my eyes away from Parker. "I'm at your mercy, sweetheart, behind bars or not. I just have one question."

She arched a brow and waited.

"After you're done being sheriff, can you keep the handcuffs?"

15

PARKER

*I*t turned out, love was forgiving. I loved that Poe had gotten himself sort-of arrested so he could apologize. I should have told them about my job. So much heartache would have been avoided. Poe wouldn't have stirred up some old shit. But love was also hard. Truths needed to be shared, fears admitted in order for it to last. Love was also all about trust.

Poe had taken mine, but I would give it back. I just wasn't sure how. I did know the four of us were most in sync when we were naked, when there was nothing between us—not work or family or jerks like Mark Beirstad.

And so I'd released Poe from jail and they'd taken me home. To *their* home. And I let them strip me bare, my clothes a pile at my feet. Nothing was said. It seemed we were all talked out. But we didn't *need* words.

They stood before me in Kemp's bedroom, their heated gazes on me. Waiting.

What did I want? What did I need?

Them.

"I love you," I said.

I did. All three of them.

"It's happened so fast. So intensely. I never thought… well, I never thought a guy would want an Amazon like me. My job. *Me.*"

"Pixie, I don't like hearing you talk negatively about yourself," Gus commented.

I gave a slight nod. "I know, but it's the truth."

"We do want you," Kemp said. "Have you ever doubted?"

"No." I looked to all three of them.

Gus. Familiar Gus. Lighthearted and sweet. Fun and my first love.

Kemp. Commanding and quiet. Focused and attentive. He saw everything, knew things about me I didn't. He pushed me to be... more.

And Poe. So big, so breakable. Intense. Fierce and ridiculously loyal.

They wanted me. *Me.*

"Can we love you?" Gus asked. "We'll kiss and touch, caress and make you come."

It sounded amazing and my nipples hardened at the idea of their hands on me. But sweet. Too sweet.

I shook my head. "That's not what I want. What I... need."

I flicked a glance at Kemp. His eyes narrowed and it seemed as if before my eyes he grew bigger, became more commanding. Dark, even though he was the fair one.

"What do you need, baby girl. Say the words."

"You."

KEMP

Her nipples hardened impossibly more. Fuck, she was gorgeous. Lush hips, full breasts, bare pussy and I could see her clit all swollen and eager for us from here. She was shivering, but I knew she wasn't cold.

She'd admitted her need to submit before. But this was different now.

Poe had bared everything, shown the open wounds of his emotions. His heart. I had a feeling that Parker would fill those places, heal them.

She needed something from all three of us. Gus's longtime love. His familiarity. My dominance, obviously. I saw her in ways Gus and Poe didn't. And Poe. She needed his protection, his fierceness. Gus and I wouldn't let anything happen to her, no fucking way, but he gave her that place where she didn't have to be fierce and brave. He'd hold those burdens for her. Keep them, and her, safe.

And her body, her desires, they belonged to us as well. She just had to hand them to us once again.

I shook my head. "Do you need to kneel before us and suck our dicks?"

She took a ragged breath, her breasts bouncing as she did so. "Yes."

"Do you need to lay back on my bed, spread your thighs and let us eat you out?"

"God, yes."

"Do you need us to tie you up, hold you down, give you your pleasure?"

"Kemp," she whimpered.

"What is it you need, baby girl?"

She licked her lips. "All three of you."

"Together?" Gus asked.

She nodded, but then remembered herself. "Yes."

"Then you'll get me in your pussy," Poe said. He hadn't spoken yet, had been cautiously waiting. I was glad he spoke now, for she was the one who would give consent.

"I'll be in your mouth," I told her. Fuck, I loved the hot suck of her mouth.

"And I'll be in your ass," Gus added.

"I never got in your ass before. It's time."

Her hand went between her thighs and she touched herself.

"Fuck, sweetheart. You need our dicks, don't you?" Poe asked, working his shirt off.

"Please," she begged.

"Oh, we'll give it to you, baby girl."

And we would. Forever.

GUS

I'd never stripped so fast in my life. Our girl was forgiving, generous, loving. And so fucking fuckable.

She wanted us at the same time. Filling her up and making her whole.

Hell, who was I kidding? She was the one making each of us whole.

Poe stripped the blanket off Kemp's bed, dropped his big frame down into the center, his head on the pillow. He curled a finger and Parker crawled up the bed and straddled him. From where I stood, I couldn't miss how wet she was. Her skin was so pale, so perfect and silky. Her breasts, generous handfuls, pressed into Kemp's bare chest as she kissed him.

Poe was tentative at first, as if he wasn't sure if he should touch her, but quickly succumbed, wrapping his arms about her and hanging on for dear fucking life.

Yeah, I knew the feeling.

Kemp opened his bedside drawer, pulled out a strip of condoms and a bottle of lube.

"You don't need those," Parker said when Poe finally let her up for air.

Kemp frowned. "Baby girl, no way will any of us take your ass without lube. We won't hurt you."

She rolled her eyes at Kemp and smiled, which only got her a light spank on her butt. "I meant the condoms."

I was in the process of climbing up on the bed when I froze. So did Poe and Kemp.

"What are you saying?" I asked.

"God, don't look so panicked. I don't want a baby or anything, at least not now. I'm on the pill and I'm clean. I just thought—mmph"

Poe kissed her, stole whatever else she was going to say. I looked to Kemp and he all but growled as he ripped off his clothes. We'd all agreed we wouldn't ever be with a woman bare until we found The One. "We" meaning Poe,

Kemp and I, but also my brothers, too. Claiming a woman raw, marking her with cum was only for the forever girl.

I told Parker that. "We take you bare, pixie, we take you forever."

She looked over her shoulder, lips swollen and slick from Poe's kisses. "I know."

Kemp tossed the condoms back into the drawer, but handed me the lube.

"You wet, sweetheart?" Poe asked. Parker gasped as he cupped her pussy. "Yeah, you are. Drenched. Good girl. Climb up on my dick then."

Moving then, she lowered herself onto him and I watched as Poe's dick disappeared into her. Bare.

"Fuck," he groaned, his hands clawing at the sheets. "I've never felt something so good. You two have got to get in her."

He didn't need to say more. Parker

fucked herself up and down a few times as I popped the top on the lube, drizzled some down and between her parted ass cheeks.

She gasped, then Poe pulled her down for a kiss. I took the opportunity to work the lube into her, pressing against her tight ring, but quickly sliding in. Tight, especially with Poe already in her. My balls ached with the need to come, especially the way she clenched down on my one finger, and then two.

Kemp put a knee on the bed. "Baby girl, you've got three holes and three men."

She lifted her head and looked to Kemp, but had to do so over the line of his dick. She grinned.

"Yes, sir."

His dick bobbed and she pressed up on her hands and took him as deep as she could.

"Fuck," he growled.

I was close to coming, and I hadn't gotten in her yet. I slipped my fingers from her, confident she was slick and loosened up. I added more lube to my palm and liberally coated my dick. Only then did Poe widen his legs, making Parker open up even more. I lined up to her back entrance and pressed in.

She moaned around Kemp and I kept going. She was still good. Tense, but trying to relax. She breathed through her nose and Poe held himself still.

I popped past that tight ring and I was in. She clenched down. Poe groaned, I bit my lip. Fuck, she was tight. Carefully, I worked my way into her, back and forth until she'd taken all of me.

Kemp stroked her hair back from her head. Praised her.

"So perfect. You're ours, Parker

Drew. Every inch of you. You belong to all three of us."

"You make us a family," I added through gritted teeth.

"I love you, sweetheart, but dudes, if you don't fucking move, I'm not going to make it."

I chuckled at that and we set a rhythm.

Poe thrust his hips up as I pulled back, fucking her in opposing motions. Kemp fucked her mouth in a slow pace, allowing her to catch her breath. Her eyes were closed, cheeks flushed as she just let go.

I saw the moment she did, felt it, for her muscles went lax and she began to whimper, to moan with the pleasure of it.

This was the ultimate submission. Pure, dirty, raw.

And when we came, Kemp first

down her throat, then me deep in her ass, and Poe marking her pussy, there was no doubt she was ours.

But more importantly, we belonged to her.

NOTE FROM VANESSA

Don't worry, there's more Grade-A Beefcakes to come!

But guess what? I've got some bonus content for you with Parker, Gus, Poe and Kemp. So sign up for my mailing list. There will be special bonus content for each Grade-A Beefcakes book, just for my subscribers. Signing up will let you hear about my next release as soon as it is out, too (and you get a free book...wow!)

As always...thanks for loving my books and the wild ride!

Vanessa

WANT MORE?

READ A SNEAK PEEK FROM PORTERHOUSE, BOOK FOUR IN THE GRADE-A BEEFCAKES SERIES.

It might be the dead of winter in Raines, Montana, but Liam and Porter will keep Jill nice and warm.

Remember: With a Vanessa Vale book, one cowboy is never enough. In this smokin' hot series, each heroine gets an extra helping (or two) of Grade-A Beefcake.

PORTERHOUSE

JILL

I could hear my cell ringing from the depths of my purse, but I wasn't taking my hands off the steering wheel to search for it, no matter how eager I was to answer. Not with the snow on the road. The latest few inches were fresh and the plows had been through, but they didn't use salt or scrape all the way down to the pavement, so the streets of Raines were a hard crust of white until the spring thaw. And that wasn't for a few more months.

A spot on the street was easy to find and I pulled in and shut off the engine. I'd been in newer models that allowed a cell phone to sync into the dashboard for hands free calling, but that wasn't something available in my older model SUV. It ran, had heat—which was great since it was close to zero—and it was mine free and clear.

I dug through my purse, found the cell. I thought it might be Porter telling me he was running late because he was coming from work in Clayton, but it was Parker Drew instead.

"You're going to talk to them, right?" she asked, not bothering with a warm up 'hello'. "No chickening out."

I rolled my eyes. "Yes. Tonight's the night."

"You sound a little panicked."

"I *am* a little panicked," I admitted. "I mean, why shouldn't I be? It's not that often a guy gets told he's not enough, and that a woman wants him *and* his best friend."

"Neither of them is going to think that," she countered.

The butterflies in my stomach were telling me otherwise. "I hope not, but it's a possibility I could end up with neither of them."

"Porter's a Duke and having two guys claim one woman is a Duke thing. I mean, look at me."

"You've got three," I corrected. She was dating—a very bland term for what she had going—Porter's cousin, Gus Duke, as well as two other guys, Kemp and Poe.

"You've been up front with them all along. It's not like anyone can get away with dating two men at the same time on the sly in a town the size of Raines without them hearing about it."

I was dating Porter Duke *and* Liam O'Malley, the new sheriff of Raines County. Right from the start, I'd told them I wanted to keep things casual. Not exclusive. Well, I was exclusively dating the two of them, but not together. I'd been interested in both of them from the very beginning, but had no idea how to tell them that. I still didn't, but tonight I was doing it anyway.

"I work too much to do anything but take it slow," I told her.

I had the hots for Porter and Liam, and I'd wanted to get to know both of them. They'd been receptive to fun, easy dates and the fact that I was going out with the other. Over the past few months, I'd been out with them, separately, to dinner, gone hiking, even bowling. Both were charming, smart, successful men—sexy, too—and I wanted both. These past few months had only confirmed that. Parker and her men proved that I could have both Porter and Liam, that my heart didn't have to settle. And she wasn't the only one. Ava, who ran the Seed and Feed, was engaged to Colton and Tucker Duke. *Two men.*

"Honey, glaciers move faster than you do," Parker added.

I frowned at her words, although she couldn't see me. We'd been friends growing up, but had lost touch over the years. She'd moved back to town a few months ago to be the temporary sheriff and we'd reconnected. The fact that she'd been Liam's boss for a few months before he was elected into the position, and the fact that she was also dating a Duke herself, made her think she was an *expert* on my dating life.

"It's one thing to casually date two

guys at once, but I draw the line at sleeping with them at the same time," I replied.

"Unless it literally is *at the same time.*"

My body heated at the idea of being the filling of a Liam and Porter sandwich. I'd fantasized about it, touched myself and climaxed at the mental picture of being in bed with the two virile men. One dark, the other fair. Big hands meant big dicks and I squirmed in my seat hoping I'd get to confirm that with them. Hopefully tonight.

"Exactly. So that's why we're meeting at Cassidy's, to tell them that I want to be with them. Together. Enough with casual dating."

"Good, because there's no doubt those two have blue balls."

"You're worried about them? What about me? Have you seen them? I've been dating two hotties and haven't gotten more than kissed."

"That's your own making," she countered. "If you'd talked to them about this weeks ago, there's no doubt in my mind you'd have gotten both of them in your bed by now."

I made a funny whimper sound. A mixture of worry, horniness and agreement.

Parker laughed. "Fix it. I've seen the way they look at you. They are into you. Seriously. Give your vibrator a break and go for the real thing. Times two."

Times two sounded fabulous. I'd never been with two guys before. My technique in bed was pretty much limited to missionary and a few other non-Kama Sutra positions. Taking on two dicks at once was well beyond my experience level. But I wanted to go for it anyway. With Porter Duke and Liam O'Malley. I wanted it all with them.

With the engine off, it was getting cold fast, but thoughts of being with those two kept me warm. Kissing them had been thrilling enough. And that had been on the mouth. What could they do to other places on my body?

My phone chimed and I looked at the screen. Another call. I didn't recognize the number.

"I've got to go," I told Parker.

"Call me tomorrow. I want all the dirty details!"

She hung up and I switched over to the other call.

"Hello?"

"Jillian Murphy?" The man's voice was deep and one I didn't recognize.

"Yes," I replied.

"This is Bob at the Jumping Jack Pawn Shop in Clayton."

All the eagerness I'd had all day for my date with Porter and Liam was gone. I stared out the front windshield at the piles of snow at the curb, the way the bright lights of the businesses on Main Street looked inviting, even in such cold weather and the way it was dark so early. Especially Cassidy's restaurant where I'd hoped to get something to eat after a long day at work—with really handsome company.

Now? Knowing what the guy was going to say? It was going to be hard to be excited about anything. Any mention of my brother, Tommy, these days was all bad and somehow involved another mess for me to clean up. My appetite for greasy cheeseburger and fries was gone.

"Yes, hi." It was rude that I didn't sound very excited to talk to Bob, but I couldn't help it.

"I'm guessing you know why I'm calling," he replied.

I leaned back against the head rest,

closed my eyes. "What did my brother pawn today?"

I held my breath.

"A TV and a rhinestone brooch shaped like a butterfly."

My mother's pin.

I gripped the steering wheel with my free hand, so tight that my knuckles were white. I envisioned it being Tommy's neck.

"While you might want a chance to get your TV back, I figured I'd give you a call about the brooch."

We'd done this once before. Last year, Tommy had taken my mother's silver tea set in and pawned it. I'd discovered it missing two days later when I'd been cleaning. I'd confronted Tommy about what he'd done and raced to the pawn shop in the hopes of getting it back. Fortunately, there wasn't a big rush for tea sets and Bob had still had it in a display case. He'd been kind and sold it back to me at the amount he'd given Tommy. I had it hidden away now in the linen closet behind the sheets. It wasn't like he ever changed his.

While my twenty-year-old brother still technically lived with me in the house we'd grown up in, I rarely saw him. He'd never had any ambition to go to college. Hell, he'd barely finished high school. He had zero work ethic and held a minimum wage job with a now-familiar irregularity. Most of his time was spent at the casino off the highway.

"Thank you," I told the pawn broker. I *was* thankful.

My anger morphed into sadness. Yes, the brooch meant something to me. Besides the house and this ancient car, there wasn't too much left that had belonged to my mother and held sentimental value. I'd had to sell quite a bit to pay for the funeral expenses and I loved that brooch.

I cleared my throat, but couldn't say anything yet.

"I'll sit it in the back," he continued. "If you want to come in, you can have it for what I gave your brother. Fifty dollars."

Fifty dollars. Tommy was giving away one of the last pieces of our mother for a measly fifty dollars. To do what? Gamble it away at the casino. The money was probably already gone.

"Yes, I'd love it if you'd hold it for me. I can come in tomorrow." I didn't have extra cash before payday, especially for something like this, but I could take it out of the food budget. It seemed it would be PB&J until next Friday.

I thanked him and ended the call.

Glancing out the window again, I saw Porter walking toward me down the sidewalk. My heart skipped a beat at the sight of him. Big, like block out the sun kind of big. Unlike his cousin who was similarly sized and went into the pro rodeo circuit, Porter had gotten a football scholarship to college. He might have left those linebacker days behind him when he graduated and went to law school, but he hadn't lost the size.

His dark hair peeked out from beneath his cowboy hat and even from a distance, I could see his dimple. He'd seen me and was smiling. At me.

God, I really liked him. No, it was a touch more than that. I was falling for him. Hard. I had a feeling he was right there with me. In fact, he wanted more of a commitment than I'd been willing to give. Not that I was a wait-for-marriage kind of gal, because I wasn't.

Glancing in the rearview mirror, I saw Liam O'Malley coming down the sidewalk from the other direction. God, my heart clenched at the sight of him as well. Laid back and easygoing, the blond had a quick smile and a generous nature. He also had pale eyes that looked at me with such heat that it ruined my panties.

But since I'd been dating both men, I refused to do more than kiss either of them, but when the chemistry was off the charts, it was soooo hard. It wouldn't be fair to do more with either one and it would feel like cheating. I didn't want to string them along, but I wanted both of them. And tonight, things had to change. No more dating. No more casual.

The men stopped in front of my car, stood shoulder to shoulder and looked at me. I gulped. This was the first time I'd seen them together. They were big, strong guys and they both wanted me.

Hopefully, after our little chat, they would continue to do so.

This was it. Two men. I wanted both of them. At the same time. And it was time to tell them.

Read Porterhouse now!

ABOUT THE AUTHOR

Vanessa Vale is the *USA Today* Bestselling author of over 50 books, sexy romance novels, including her popular Bridgewater historical romance series and hot contemporary romances featuring unapologetic bad boys who don't just fall in love, they fall hard. When she's not writing, Vanessa savors the insanity of raising two boys and figuring out how many meals she can make with a pressure cooker. While she's not as skilled at social media as her kids, she loves to interact with readers.

BookBub

Instagram

www.vanessavaleauthor.com
facebook.com/vanessavaleauthor
instagram.com/vanessa_vale_author

Hitched

Lassoed

Bridgewater County Series

Ride Me Dirty

Claim Me Hard

Take Me Fast

Hold Me Close

Make Me Yours

Kiss Me Crazy

Mail Order Bride of Slate Springs Series

A Wanton Woman

A Wild Woman

A Wicked Woman

Bridgewater Ménage Series

Their Runaway Bride

Their Kidnapped Bride

Their Wayward Bride

Their Captivated Bride

Their Treasured Bride

Their Christmas Bride

Their Reluctant Bride

Their Stolen Bride

Their Brazen Bride

Their Bridgewater Brides- Books 1-3
Boxed Set

Outlaw Brides Series

Flirting With The Law

MMA Fighter Romance Series

Fight For Her

Wildflower Bride Series

Rose

Hyacinth

Dahlia

Daisy

Lily

Montana Men Series

The Lawman

The Cowboy

The Outlaw

Standalone Reads

Twice As Delicious

Western Widows

Sweet Justice

Mine To Take

Relentless

Sleepless Night

Man Candy - A Coloring Book

CPSIA information can be obtained
at www.ICGtesting.com
Printed in the USA
BVHW080824220719
554058BV00007B/236/P